TAKEN BY THE STORM PRINCE

HAVEN ACADEMY: BOOK 2

ARIEL RENNER

CONTENTS

CHAPTER ONE

Hopelessness hung in the air like a thick fog through the vast halls of the Ice Castle. As sunlight gleamed through the translucent blue walls of the tower that had been home for my entire life, a biting cold crept into my skin and bones like never before. All around me was nothing but a haunting silence, like time had stopped, broken only by my own desperate pleas.

"Mother, please," I begged, my voice trembling. "There must be another way."

My mother, the Ice Queen, stood regally before me in a gown of shimmering frost, her frigid blue gaze as cold and unyielding as steel. Her pale face expressed nothing. A crown of spiked icicles rested atop her long white hair, similar to my own, that cascaded like a frozen waterfall down her back. The air around her smelled of winter, like the smell of freshly fallen snow or the crispness of a breeze. There was no warmth in my mother's embrace, just a statue of cold marble and the icy mask of indifference.

Her reserved voice echoed through the grand hall like a death sentence.

"Your marriage to the Storm Prince has been settled," she said, resolute and unmoved. "It's time for you to go to your new family."

Tears streamed down my face as my happiness slipped away. While my parents approved of my betrothal, my older brother, Fannar, warned all of us about the Storm Prince, that he was a monster—violent and ruthless. The fate before me was unbearable. Being forced to marry a tyrant like the Storm Prince was akin to being held captive forever.

I knew I had no choice but to obey my mother, but still, hope lingered in my heart. With utmost sincerity, I looked at my mother and asked her one last time, begging her to find another way—some other form of salvation for us both.

"I can't marry him, Mother!" I cried out desperately. "He is cruel. He will beat me and treat me like a slave. Please, don't make me go!"

"I've already explained this to you, Gwyneira," she said, exasperated. "Tensions between the kingdoms of the Enchanted Realm have never been greater. Our kingdom needs allies if we want a chance at surviving a war with another kingdom. We need to form an alliance with the Storm Kingdom, and this is the only way."

The despair that descended upon me was almost too much to bear, crushing my soul underneath its overwhelming weight. I wailed and collapsed to my knees in surrender. No matter how much I pleaded, there was no escaping the dire future that awaited me.

"Your behavior is unbecoming of a princess!" my mother scolded. "It is an honor for you to fulfill this duty to our kingdom."

She turned to my ladies-in-waiting, who were silently lined up against the wall. "Adis, take Gwyneira to her room. Get her cleaned up and pack her belongings. We leave for the Storm Kingdom in an hour."

Adis stepped forward. "Yes, Your Majesty."

She came over first, followed by my two other ladies. They gripped both of my arms and led me like a rag doll out of the room and up the stairs toward my bedroom.

The quill quivered as I pressed it to the paper. I wiped the tears from my cheeks as quickly as I could. After cleaning me up, Adis had just applied fresh makeup. I didn't want my mother to make her do it again.

The letter was already dotted with little spider webs of ink from where saltwater hit the page. If I wanted to send Fannar a letter, he needed to be able to read it.

I read it one more time:

My dearest brother,

This might be the last letter you receive from me. Mother and Father have finalized my betrothal to the Storm Prince, and I'm moments from being sent to the Storm Kingdom—maybe forever.

I wish they would at least wait until you were back from the academy so I could say goodbye face to face.

I am so scared. I am so scared of my new fiancé. I know about his reputation but fear how much worse he will be behind closed doors. You always said to be strong. I will be as brave as I can, but I need your help. Fannar, please save me from this monster!

Praying that we see each other again soon,

Gwyneira

A knock sounded at my door.

"Yes?" I asked.

Adis opened the door, curtsied, and clasped her hands in front of her. "Princess, it's time."

"Thank you, Adis. I am coming."

She hurried into my room to grab the last few items on my bed and waited near the doorway.

I folded the letter and handed it to her. "Please ensure this reaches my brother."

"I will, Princess." She paused to look at me one last time. "You look lovely, Your Highness."

Adis had dressed me in a beautiful ice-blue gown for my first meeting with my betrothed. It sparkled like diamonds as the thousands of crystals sewn into the dress reflected the light, capturing every color of the rainbow. The light and airy fabric draped softly over the length of my body with an elaborate shimmering, translucent overlay that trailed behind me on the floor.

"Thank you, Adis." I clasped her hands. "For everything."

Her soft blue eyes began to glisten, and her lips curved up in a gentle but pained smile. "If it's not out of place . . . I'm going to miss you so much! It has been a pleasure serving you, Your Highness."

More tears pricked at my eyes. "I'm going to miss you too." I threw my arms around her and embraced her.

She hugged me back and gave the lightest sob into my shoulder. "Happy birthday, Princess," she said quietly. "I am so sorry."

I'd known my eighteenth birthday would bring misery. My parents had made it clear that as both the second child and a female, I was a burden on our family. But nothing could have prepared me for the soul-crushing loneliness of losing my home, my brother, and all that I had ever known to be traded away to a monster. The pain was worse than any torture, digging deep into my heart and leaving me hollowed out and utterly alone.

Yet I still had a duty to my kingdom—a duty to meet my fate.

Before I knew it, I found myself thrust into the royal carriage with my parents, listening to the clip-clopping of the ice unicorns and watching the snow-white kingdom pass me by.

The Ice Kingdom was a winter wonderland. Powder covered the pine trees year-round, and most buildings, including our castle, were made of shining cerulean ice.

My home. This might be the last time I see it . . .

"Stop making that face," Mother barked at me. "It's unbecoming of an Ice Princess."

My thoughts must have given way to a sad look on my face. I took a deep breath and released it slowly.

Emotions are weakness.

Since Fannar and I were born, our parents drilled into our heads that emotions are a sign of weakness. As royalty, we could never show weakness, especially in the presence of outsiders.

"Do not forget your place, young lady," Father grunted. "Especially once you are on your own in the Storm Kingdom. We have a reputation you must uphold."

I nodded, praying the tears wouldn't begin to flow again. Father would slap me if they did. With a stern face, the Ice King's piercing blue eyes bore into me with disdain. He wore a crisp navy-blue military dress uniform adorned with gold buttons and countless medals pinned to the chest. Atop his head of short, silver hair, he wore an intricately crafted crown of latticed ice that sparkled in the sunlight.

Both of them had the same expression they always did: complete dispassion, like statues. I couldn't remember my parents ever looking any other way.

"Will I ever get to come back?" I asked quietly, fighting to keep emotion off my face.

Mother looked down her razor-sharp nose at me. "That depends on the Storm Prince. I suppose if you are a good wife, he will allow you to visit. Regardless, the Storm Kingdom will be your home now, so you'd best get accustomed to it."

"But I never said goodbye to Fannar."

"Stop acting like a child," Father admonished. "Both you and the prince must fulfill your royal duties to the kingdom. His education at Haven Academy will make him a stronger and more formidable king. You will secure our alliance with the Storm Kingdom. Be proud, Gwyneira. You are protecting our people from harm."

"Y-yes, Father."

"No more crying," Mother snapped. "You need to earn the Storm Prince's favor. No one will want you if your face is swollen and ugly from crying."

I sunk down in my seat and linked my hands together, crushing my knuckles in my grip as I tried to memorize the winter wonderland that spread outside the window one last time.

The unicorns pulled our carriage through a portal swirling with black magic. In a second, we were on the other side, entering the Storm Kingdom, the light vanishing as soon as we did. The pleasant blue sky, occasionally broken by steely gray clouds dropping peaceful snowflakes, was suddenly as dark as night and filled with growling black clouds, threatening violence. Miles of gloomy trees lined the road, the kind story books would describe as "the wrong way" in a dark, enchanted forest.

As the alien environment surrounded us, my anxiety heightened, as if the gloomy change just reaffirmed that my new life would be filled with despair.

The Storm Castle began to appear in my window of the carriage. A black spiked fortress loomed before us. Razor-sharp towers jutted out in every direction, like brambles growing hundreds of feet high, casting ominous shadows on the ground below. It looked horrifying—but it fit in with what I thought awaited me there: a twisted and dangerous place filled with terrors beyond imagination.

The large black gates opened and then clanked shut behind us, trapping us inside. Thorn bushes lined the pathway, wickedly beckoning the carriage forward with their eerie branches.

As we stopped in front of the castle, greeters in black opened the door of our carriage, and I stepped out, blinking at how dark yet warm the weather was.

"This way, Princess." One of the greeters gestured to me.

They led us inside and through several rooms. Each one of them was dimly lit by a few lanterns valiantly fighting the darkness, but that somehow made it eerier.

Soon, we were in a large hall with two very imposing figures, a man and a woman, each sitting on their own throne. The Storm King's tanned face sported a very unusual beard in black ringlets, and a shiny gold crown contrasted his curly black hair. His military dress uniform was black and trimmed in knotted gold rope.

The Storm Queen had a powerful and captivating appearance. She wore an elegant, long black dress adorned with gold embroidery that added to her commanding presence. Around her neck hung a gold necklace with a charm in the shape of thunderbolts. The diamonds and rubies of her golden tiara glinted in the lantern light of the throne room. Her long raven hair cascaded down her back, and her complexion was almost as pale as Mother's. Her stern and stoic face also reminded me of Mother as well, but the mystery in her midnight eyes made me afraid that she could somehow curse me with black magic.

The sulking figure of a large young man sat on the steps leading up to the thrones. Prince Brontes wore a black military dress uniform like his father but with fewer medals. He stared at the floor with his eyebrows knitted together and mouth pressed tight. One arm was folded in front of him, while the other rested on his knee, his hand clutching his chin.

"Brontes, get up!" The Storm Queen commanded him in a hushed tone.

The prince bolted to his feet, and his piercing navy eyes glared at me from underneath his shaggy black hair. A shudder rolled through my body, my skin prickling from his gaze. He surveyed me for an endless moment before his lip curled and he looked away.

"Your Majesties and Your Royal Highness." The greeter bowed before the thrones. "May I present Their Majesties, the King and Queen of the Ice Kingdom, and Her Royal Highness, the Princess of the Ice Kingdom."

The Storm King and Queen stood up from their thrones out of courtesy. "Welcome to the Storm Kingdom."

"Thank you for having us," Father said.

The Storm Queen descended from her throne and began to inspect me so closely that her long hair brushed my face. Her fingers grabbed my chin and tilted it up toward her.

"Pretty face," she remarked without any warmth.

"Tha—" I began to say.

"But very skinny," she cut me off and furrowed her eyebrows.

"As was her mother," Father replied. "Yet she still bore two children."

Ew.

"Hm," the Storm Queen grunted. "And how are her powers?"

"They have not manifested yet," Mother replied. "But if the Ice Prince is any indication, she will be powerful."

"We don't allow the use of powers at court. She will need to keep them under strict control no matter how powerful she becomes."

"Well, she is your responsibility now," Father replied.

My heart shrank little by little as my own parents talked about me like I was livestock. I wanted to crawl into a corner and die.

The Storm Queen smiled, and it caught me off guard. Reading other people's emotions was something I always had trouble with. Emotions were a sign of weakness in the Ice Kingdom. Very seldom had I seen so many people in one room, let alone anything but ice-cold expressions around me.

Why is she smiling? Do they just smile often in the Storm Kingdom or is there a reason? Is it good or bad that she's smiling?

"Very well," the Storm Queen said at last. "We accept her."

Mother let out a light sigh of relief. "That is good to hear."

"If we are in agreement, let us make the final arrangements." The Storm King finally spoke.

"Yes, then we can be on our way," Father agreed. "There is business in the Ice Kingdom we must attend to."

"Brontes, why don't you get acquainted with the princess?" the Storm Queen said to him before adding, "But don't leave this room until we get back."

"This way to my study." The Storm King, followed by the Storm Queen, led my parents out of the throne room.

The throne room was eerily silent after our parents' departure. I inhaled a deep breath, the butterflies in my stomach fluttering wildly as I studied the Storm Prince closer. He looked so handsome and dashing in his military dress uniform, like a prince right out of a fairy tale. Those deep navy-blue eyes were as mysterious as his mother's but set with a strong jawline and massive neck. He towered over me by at least six to eight inches, and the uniform could barely contain his bulging biceps as he crossed them over his broad chest. My heartbeat quickened as my eyes followed their curves. A jolt ran through me at the thought of what lay beneath that fabric.

Suddenly, I realized those dark eyes were roaming over my body with a boldness that made my mind race and my heart squirm. I couldn't tell if he was sizing me up like he would an enemy.

I quickly averted my view, not wanting to be caught staring. But when I dared to look back up, the storm brewing in his eyes made me both nervous and excited.

"I guess you'll do," he said gruffly with a grin. The deep rumble of his voice sent shivers down my spine. Was he trying to make a joke?

As much as I didn't want to admit it, there was something about him that was both alluring and dangerous. His piercing gaze bore into mine, causing something to stir inside me. I never wanted this engagement, but I thought maybe it might work—for the sake of our kingdoms, and maybe for the sake of my own happiness—at least for a fleeting moment.

He paused and narrowed his eyes at me. "Look, I don't want to be engaged either. I have no interest in marrying you, let alone being in the same room as you. But it's our duty to our families and our kingdoms. We might hate each other, but we don't need to make it worse than it has to be."

Hate each other? Does he hate me already?

His choice of words stabbed me with an unexpected pang of hurt since I'd barely known him for fifteen minutes, but I refused to let him see it. I shook the desire to speak out of my head, knowing I must remain resolute in my role as the Ice Princess. My heart pounded, my palms were sweaty, and yet I refused to let myself give into the turmoil inside me. I had to stay composed and emotionless, something that seemed increasingly difficult by the second.

"What's wrong with you?" he snapped suddenly. "Can't you talk?"

The stories of the prince's wrath swirled in my thoughts, and fear of the monster I had heard about washed over me, causing me to flinch and step back from him. Was he going to hurt me?

His voice grew even louder. "Forget it, then!" He stomped back up the stairs toward the thrones, then crossed his arms, staring at the wall. "I knew this was going to be awful," he muttered.

He seemed to be simmering with rage, and I had no idea how to deal with it. I remained standing in the grand hall, staring at his back, feeling more alone than ever before.

The clacking of the Storm Queen's high heels echoed throughout the grand hall, breaking the stifling silence between us long before she returned to the throne room. Her expression now was unforgiving and cold.

"I will take her from here, Brontes," she said as she waved him away. "Go back to your duties."

"Yes, Mother," he responded and left without another glance at me.

"Where are my parents?" I asked.

"They've already left," she answered and sat down on her throne.

My parents just left me without saying goodbye?

My heart sank to the bottom of my feet.

The Storm Queen turned to the guards. "One of you, fetch Maisol." She then turned to me. "Maisol is the Kitchen Head. She will be showing you around your new home, ice girl."

"Yes, Your Majesty," I murmured.

"Do not speak unless I ask you a direct question!"

Her suddenly harsh tone startled me. I wanted to shrink and hide.

She continued sternly, "You may be considered important where you come from, but here, you will need to prove yourself worthy of the prince."

I nodded quietly.

"That's more like it."

A servant girl appeared and curtsied before the queen. "Yes, Your Majesty?"

"Maisol, show the ice girl to the servants' quarters and put her to work in the morning." The queen turned to me. "You'll be living in the servants' quarters until you convince me that you won't embarrass our family."

My heart sank even further. *The servants' quarters? Are they really going to treat me like a servant?*

"You will also start your tutorship in Storm etiquette and culture under my teaching tomorrow. Now, go!"

I stood stunned. Maisol took me by the hand and dragged me out of the throne room, out of the entire castle, and into what was essentially a large old barn tucked behind the castle, next to the stables. Inside, there were two dozen rickety old beds and a steamer trunk in front of each bed, which I assumed were for personal items and clothing.

"Here we are, Your Royal Highness, the girls' quarters," Maisol said. "Your bed is the furthest one to the right. Your nightgown and work clothes are in the trunk." She looked me up and down. "They might be a little big for you, but I think you can make it work. Get to bed. You'll be required to get up at five o'clock like the rest of us." She turned to leave.

"Where are you going?" I asked.

"Dinner service. Enjoy your night off. It'll be your last one for a long time."

With that, she left, and I was truly alone. I couldn't hold the tears back any longer. I threw myself onto my rickety, musty bed and sobbed away the remainder of my eighteenth birthday.

CHAPTER TWO

It was an uneasy night, but it was over before I knew it. At five o'clock the next morning, before the sun had even risen, and I was trading in my beautiful crystal gown for a servant's uniform.

"Good morning, Your Royal Highness," Maisol greeted me with a big smile. "I'm impressed. The royal family wouldn't be able to wake up this early if their lives depended on it!"

She was a little firecracker of a woman—dark hair that looked black until the light caught it just right and gave it a shimmer of navy, with a stocky and strong figure that was clearly accustomed to labor. She would almost be intimidating if the smile that lifted her big round cheeks didn't seem—from what I could tell—entirely genuine.

"Good morning, Maisol," I replied, trying to be cheerful. "Please call me, Gwyneira."

"Okay, Gwyneira. Her Majesty the Queen said that you need to learn to cook and clean with us."

I nodded and followed Maisol to the basement of the castle.

As we entered the expansive kitchen, it was already bustling with twenty-something servants preparing a mighty breakfast for the royal family. Inside was very humid—almost unbearably hot for an Ice Enchanted like me. There weren't any windows among the stone walls, so the smell of years of cooking oil saturated the air so thickly that I could taste it. There must have been a hundred drawers and cabinets, all covered in an unappealing layer of grease, lining the kitchen walls.

Maisol walked me over to one of the counters. "Since you're new, we'll start off with something easy. How about you peel these potatoes?" She gestured to a large bowl of brown potatoes and handed me a short bladed utensil.

"I . . . okay . . ." I stuttered, gaping at the odd device as I took it. I had no idea what it was or how to use it.

"Are you sure?" She arched an eyebrow at me.

No emotions. No weakness. "Absolutely," I replied.

As she turned away, I slowly put the bladed . . . *thing* onto the potato and drew it across. Nothing happened.

Maybe I just need to use a little more force. I yanked the blade over the potato and—

"OW!" I yelped.

"Gwyneira!" Maisol exclaimed.

"Oh, for gods' sake!" another girl groaned across the kitchen. "She's absolutely useless!"

"You need to be careful, or you'll bleed all over the queen's food." Maisol smirked.

After checking to make sure I was not, in fact, bleeding, she patiently showed me how to properly peel a potato. I eventually got the hang of it after my fifth or sixth one. However, by the time breakfast was plated and handed over to the waiters, numerous tiny lacerations covered my hands. Still, I reveled in the accomplishment of learning something new. Perhaps tomorrow, I could master shaving the peel into the trash can instead of onto the floor.

When Maisol saw my hands, she tsk-tsked at me with a smile before bringing me to the sink to wash them off. She chuckled. "Wow, you truly haven't done anything like this before, have you?"

I didn't react, staring at her cluelessly. Wrapping my head around an environment where people smiled and frowned was hard enough. I couldn't imagine forming an expression in response.

"Don't worry," she said. "It's your first day."

Suddenly, a voice called over the pair of us. "Why does a princess need to learn how to cook and clean, anyway?"

"Yes, what is the point? She's going to be waited upon hand and foot like that spoiled prince!"

"Well, perhaps *she* will be the one waiting hand and foot on him!"

They burst into laughter. An unusual rage rattled through my body as I assumed they were mocking Fannar.

But before I could say anything, Maisol shushed the others. "Quiet! Do you know what will happen to us if the queen hears you talking about her son that way?"

"Please!" Rori retorted. "One of the queen's handmaids told me that the queen herself calls the prince a monster because his Enchanted Mark is tainted."

That's right. Fannar isn't the resident prince here.

"Brontes?" I asked.

"Well, he is the queen's son, isn't he?" Maisol retorted while turning to me. "Oh, yeah. He's your fiancé now, isn't he?" She smirked, as if questioning whether she could trust me with their backhanded comments about the royals. "Well, he *is* spoiled, like Rori said. To be honest, we thought we'd be waiting on *you* hand and foot as well, not working with you down here."

An odd chill coursed through me as the warm water enveloped my hands. My heart raced, and I sensed a peculiar energy coursing through my body, momentarily making me feel light-headed. What was happening to me?

Beneath the water, my hands began to assume a translucent light blue hue and small flecks of frost gathered around my fingertips.

I withdrew my hands from the sink, only to discover them encased in clumps of ice.

Huh, go figure. My ice powers finally manifested after peeling potatoes in the Storm Castle of all places.

Maisol gawked at my frozen hands for a moment before quickly covering them with a towel. The ice shattered immediately upon contact.

"Do not let the queen see you do that!" Maisol urgently hissed. "She will beat you black and blue if she does!"

I looked up at her curiously. "She said that powers were forbidden in the court. Why is that?"

Maisol shrugged. "I'm not entirely sure. The queen says that Storm powers are too powerful and volatile to be mastered, so everyone is banned from using them here. But . . ." She gained an odd expression, a half-smile, and continued. "I've seen the knights training in magic, so we think there's a cover-up."

"What would she be covering up?"

"Who knows? The servants aren't exactly in any position to figure it out." She turned away. "Come. We're allowed to eat the leftovers now the royal family has been fed."

I smiled at her. No matter the implicit insult of eating leftovers, what the servants had made smelled divine, and I was getting quite hungry. We ate at a huge communal table in the middle of the food storage room next to the kitchen.

As I shoveled the last bite of food into my mouth, a female voice called from the kitchen entryway. "Princess?"

An older woman wearing a pretty gray velvet dress looked at me from the kitchen entryway.

"Yes?" I answered.

"Good morning, Princess. I'm the Storm Queen's lady-in-waiting. Her Majesty the Queen is requesting your presence."

As I stood up, I passed a glance to Maisol, Rori, and the others, and their soft eyes looked back at me with what I believed was sympathy.

I followed the woman through the castle into a room I'd never seen before. It appeared to be a drawing room. The Storm Queen stood waiting in the middle of the room, holding a long ruler.

I bowed once I entered the room. "Your Majesty."

"Ice girl," she said. "It's time for your first etiquette lesson."

As her lady-in-waiting left, closing the door behind her, the queen surveyed me, folding her arms with the same look she had the day before. I began to recognize it as disdain.

"I *still* think you are too skinny," she grunted at me. "But I suppose you'll do. Now, stand up straight and let me look at you properly."

I straightened my back for her, and she scoffed at me again. "No, *straight!* Like a lady!"

I did not know what she was talking about, so I made a vague gesture to show I wanted to speak, and she smiled at me. But it was a different smile than I knew from Maisol and Rori—or indeed, Fannar. It came with sharp eyes and sunken eyebrows. It was a darker smile. A bad one.

"At least you learn quickly. Speak."

"Forgive me, but what do you mean by 'straight,' Your Majesty?"

She nodded at me, that same grim smile on her face.

"Well, I shouldn't be surprised. You disgusting Ice Enchanted act like you're better than us, but clearly, you belong in the barn, since you were raised in one. It's obvious that Storm Enchanted are far superior." The queen approached me, then suddenly pinched my cheek—hard—as she did. "But don't worry. I'll make a lady out of you soon enough, even if you are a miserable Ice Enchanted."

She left and returned with a book. A large and heavy one.

"So, 'straight' means you'll be able to carry this book atop your head and not allow it to fall. We will not be leaving this room until you can walk the length of it without dropping the book."

It was more challenging than it sounded. I couldn't walk more than three steps without the book tumbling down. Every time it happened, the Storm Queen smacked me with the ruler, usually on my wrists or the back of my arms, but after one particularly embarrassing performance, she hit the back of my thighs. Every time I was struck, the sting made me yelp, and she would tell me to be quiet.

Be strong, Gwyneira, Fannar's voice comforted me in my head.

Then, all of a sudden, it seemed to click. The book stopped falling, and I walked back and forth as though it was stuck to my head. There was a cold tingling throughout my body as I walked, I was concentrating so hard.

The queen's smile changed—I was beginning to recognize the difference between her smiles—the raised eyebrows and softer eyes.

"Good!" she said, more approvingly. "We may be able to move on faster than I thought."

I gestured my desire to talk again.

"Speak."

"If it isn't rude to ask, Your Majesty, why aren't powers allowed in court?"

Her facial expression darkened, so I added, "I-I'm not questioning you. I only want to understand."

The Storm Queen sighed. "I realize you may have difficulty understanding this concept, being an Ice Enchanted, but the powers of storm and ice are starkly different. Our powers are wild, unpredictable, and deadly. If not suppressed, people get hurt."

"Deadly?" I asked.

Her eyes were sharp again. "Yes, all it would take is one stray bolt of lightning for Brontes to kill you. He's almost killed someone before, and it could easily happen again."

Brontes almost killed someone?

Suddenly, a monstrous crash rattled throughout the entire castle. I whipped around to look for the source, but it was on the other side of a wall.

"Speak of the devil," the queen sighed.

"That's . . . that was Brontes?" I gasped.

She didn't answer me. Instead, she looked up at my head, and that disdainful expression came back *tenfold.* She strode over and grabbed the book from on top of my head. When she wrenched it off, I shrieked in pain, feeling a good chunk of my white hair being ripped off with it. When the Storm Queen looked under the book, where the hair still clung, she saw the patch of ice it was attached to.

"You were cheating, you little witch!" She snarled at me. "You dare try to deceive the *Storm Queen*?!"

"N-no, I didn't! I didn't mean to!" I stuttered.

The queen then drew the long ruler back and struck me across the face. I stumbled backward as searing pain exploded across my face.

I barely managed to keep from falling. Iron-sharp blood filled my mouth and flowed from my nose. But it froze before dripping to the ground.

The queen's dark eyes glared at me even more. They were burning. "You are *still doing it!*"

"No, not on purpose, Your Majesty! I swear!"

She raised the ruler again, and I covered my head.

Be strong, Gwyneira, Fannar's voice urged me again. *Be brave.*

I stifled my tears and screams as pain scattered across my body over and over again. *Show no emotion. Show no weakness.* I couldn't remember how long it lasted, but I was grateful when she finally dismissed me.

Outside, I finally allowed myself to shed a few tears. My legs struggled to carry me as I stumbled back toward the servants' quarters. The short stroll felt like the longest hike.

A single thought repeated in my mind: *I just . . . need to make it back . . . to the servants' quarters . . .*

When I arrived back at the barn, I wiped my tears away. *Show no emotion. Show no weakness.* As I struggled to open the door, the chattering from within the room grew quiet. Eventually, one of the servants I'd only seen in passing before then opened the door. His eyes widened.

"Shit." He turned to shout over his shoulder. "Maisol, I think you'd better deal with this!"

I was relieved to hear her name, and soon, Maisol appeared at the door. "Oh, my gods! Are you okay?"

I nodded. "I think the bleeding has stopped."

Maisol sighed and pulled me inside. "Let's get you cleaned up." A small smile spread across her face. "After that, you want to play a card game with us? It might make you feel a bit better."

For the first time since I got there, a small smile twitched at the corners of my lips. "Yes, please."

CHAPTER THREE

Life in the Storm Castle wasn't easy for me, but oddly, acting as one of the help was somehow easier than trying to be a princess. I slept in the barn with all the servant girls, and we awoke at five o'clock every morning, usually before the sun had risen or the roosters crowed. We sleepily dressed ourselves and headed outside to the water spigots to wash our faces and hands.

"Brr!" Rori shivered. "I *hate* these damn things! The water is always freezing!" She would say something like that almost every morning, and Maisol would roll her eyes and smile. I learned to do the same. Rori was a very slender woman with slim fingers and looked almost skin and bone. Despite that, she was the fiercest of the girls I met, except when it came to cold water, apparently.

As they often did, the servant boys emerged from their own barn and started vying for the water spigots as well.

"Ah!" Elias sighed. "Don't you just love mornings?"

"No, just you!" Dagur snapped back before giving me a smile. "What about you, ice girl?" he said, pulling me into the conversation. "You must like mornings—they're really cold!"

Elias laughed and watched me for a moment for my reaction.

"Oh . . . um, yes," I answered quietly. "Mornings are beautiful."

Elias worked in the stables, and his body reflected a lifetime of hauling hay: big muscles from head to toe and short sandy blond hair dusted with hay dust. He was always perky in the mornings, as opposed to Dagur, who always seemed to be barely awake until midday. Dagur was a chef, so perhaps it was the lunch rush that woke him up. Dagur's occupation was also reflected in his form—a lean body and broad fingers, blunted from years of kitchen work.

After washing up, we went our separate ways to our assigned duties. Once the work was done, the servants gathered together in one barn or the other and wiled their evenings away. Sometimes, they played card games, shared castle gossip, and munched on leftovers together. Occasionally, they even practiced their powers, which surprised me—the queen was so firm about not using powers in court that it was incredible to see Storm Enchanted in action.

For the most part, the entire group welcomed me and treated me like one of them. A few even took me through some breathing exercises and encouraged me to use my newly manifested powers. I knew it was because they just wanted to see my ice, but I was grateful for the chance to practice. I had never experienced any of this before in the Ice Castle, where my only company was Adis, especially after Fannar went to the academy. I'd never been with a *group* of people that were just laughing, joking, having animated conversations, and throwing their powers at each other for fun.

I was getting better at reading their facial expressions as well, unlearning the lifetime of impassivity I was taught in the Ice Kingdom and learning which smiles meant what and which expression with scrunched eyebrows was a disapproving frown and which was concern for my well-being. I received the latter quite a bit when I spoke of my time in the Ice Castle—apparently, being kept in a tower constantly, taught nothing, and allowed nowhere wasn't an existence any of them could comprehend being the slightest bit enjoyable. But I was just happy to be with them, finally accepted into a group of people I could call my friends with absolute certainty.

I did my best to learn quickly, as I didn't want to be a burden on the only friends I had.

They taught me how to do nearly all my chores, and they even helped me pass my etiquette sessions with the Storm Queen—practicing balancing the book on my head or curtsying correctly in the servants' quarters late at night after all the work was done. Even though she still took every opportunity to insult me and my kingdom, she soon allowed me more freedom in the castle. Not as much as a member of the royal family, but what a regular member of the staff would be allowed, and that gave me the opportunity to explore a little.

When I first saw the Storm Castle, it seemed to stretch on forever, an imposing, dark fortress with oppressive walls that loomed over me like a menacing mountain. But once I had a chance to take in details, those foreboding walls revealed unexpected intricate carvings in dark cherry wood of birds, flowers, and trees, along with scenes depicting rain, thunderstorms, and sun. The castle wasn't as ghastly as I had first feared.

Instead of the eternal wintery stillness I'd grown accustomed to in the Ice Kingdom, the air here was alive and brisk. The sky shifted from azure blue to onyx black. Puffy white clouds turned to slate before releasing rain or hail onto the land below.

It wasn't gloomy here all the time, as I had originally thought. Even when storms descended over the castle, they soon yielded, unveiling sunrays that danced on dew-covered blades of grass and glistened off puddles that stretched in sparkling reflections into a distant horizon. Though thunderstorms were a common occurrence, they were a comforting reminder that even in darkness there can be beauty.

From the high castle towers, the magnificent landscape of the Storm Kingdom stretched before me, an endless panorama of beauty. Unrelenting gusts swept through an endless canopy of vibrant treetops that desperately clung to their verdant foliage. Peaceful meadows splayed across the rolling hills like a vivid quilt dotted with wildflowers that blossomed amidst each storm

and burst into brilliant hues of yellow, red, and blue. Their petals danced in vibrant swirls as the breeze swept through them.

The sunsets were beyond anything I had ever seen in pictures. The horizon glowed with pinkish-orange clouds that shaded the rolling hills below. The tops of distant trees were illuminated in golden light as their shadows stretched out along the grassy plains. The setting sun painted the sky with delicate hues, mixing into bright purples and deep blues that shimmered above me. Even when wisps of fog drifted through the landscape, it was still breathtakingly beautiful and magical, as if each evening brought something different and special, another glimpse of a world I had only dreamed about before.

Every night, as I walked between the castle and the servants' quarters, I would pause and cast my gaze up at the night sky. The stars twinkled in the darkness, scattered across an endless expanse of inky velvet like diamonds. Diligently applying my knowledge of astronomy, acquired from devouring countless books on the subject, I identified the stars and constellations overhead. Standing beneath their shimmering beauty, they captivated me, surpassing the view I had from the window of my tower in the Ice Castle. Each night filled me with wonder, inviting me to explore the universe. No matter how many times I peered up at the stars, their breathtaking beauty never failed to steal my breath away, humbling and inspiring me with the vastness of the cosmos.

The chandelier above cast a warm glow as I ran my duster across the ornate wooden bookshelf, sending particles of dust dancing in the air. The opulent palace library had become one of my favorite places to clean since arriving at the Storm Castle two weeks prior. Ancient tomes and scrolls filled its floor-to-ceiling shelves. From the far corner of the library where I stood, I had an excellent view of a cloudy mid-afternoon sky through the tall windows. The scent of old parchment, wood polish, and leather filled my nostrils as I continued my task.

I remembered how grateful I would be when Fannar used to sneak one or two books into my room, allowing me to escape the confines of my tower and explore the world beyond its walls. I never dreamed of seeing thousands upon thousands of books like this. *Be careful not to damage any of these precious books, Gwyn.* I thought to myself, recalling the stern warning from the castle's head housekeeper. These were the treasures of the Storm Kingdom, after all.

As I carefully brushed the duster along a row of book spines, the heavy oak doors creaked open, and my eyes darted toward the entrance. Prince Brontes strode into the room with intent. His stormy gray eyes intensely scanned the vast collection of books like they were searching for prey.

My heart skipped a beat. I'd barely seen him since my first day in the castle, and I hadn't spoken to him since then either. I quickly averted my gaze and attempted to focus on my duties, hoping he wouldn't notice me all the way in the back of the library.

Brontes huffed under his breath with frustration. He paced around the room, the pounding of his boots echoing against the marble floor. One moment, he appeared calm and collected. The next, his brows furrowed, and he cursed quietly, as if attempting to contain a tempest within him.

My mind began to wander as I watched him from the corner of my eye. Despite my better judgment, I found myself fascinated by him. He had a noble aura about him, and yet there was something almost wild in his energy, like an animal pacing in its cage.

His strong arms reached for a book on a high shelf, and an unfamiliar warmth stirred within me. His unruly mane of dark hair cascaded over his forehead, making me want to run my fingers through it. The impossibly broad expanse of his shoulders stretched taut against the fabric of his shirt. For a moment, I wanted nothing more than to feel the power of those strong arms under my fingertips, but I promptly reminded myself that he was a monster.

I quickly snapped myself out of it and shook my head to clear my thoughts. I couldn't imagine what the queen would do if I was caught daydreaming in the presence of the prince and *fantasizing about him,* no less! I scolded myself silently as I resumed dusting the shelves with more vigor than necessary.

"Ah, there it is!" he exclaimed a few minutes later, finally spotting his desired book.

His sudden outburst startled me, and my duster clattered to the floor. I winced. *So much for going unnoticed.*

Brontes turned sharply and demanded, "Who's there?"

I stepped forward so he could see me. "It's me, Your Highness," I said quietly, being sure to keep my eyes downcast and my voice as flat as possible, not to give away a hint of emotion. "I apologize if I disturbed you."

"No need to apologize, Princess," he said. "You weren't disturbing me. Have you been hiding here all along?"

"Not hiding." I bent down to retrieve the fallen duster. "Just dusting."

The thudding of his boots grew louder as he approached me. Inwardly, I braced myself, not knowing what to expect from him. When I straightened up, he was so close that I could feel the heat emanating from his body, and I froze in place.

"Well, you've done an excellent job dusting." His lips turned upward ever so slightly.

His gaze swept across the length of my body from the floor to my face, where it lingered for what felt like an eternity before finally meeting mine. His stormy blue eyes bore into me, probing deep into my soul.

My heart raced as I stared back at him, perplexed by his expression. Was his compliment genuine, or had he been mocking me, knowing full well that I was a princess being treated like a servant? Why did he look at me with such intensity? My head spun with questions muddled by uncertainty and confusion as I tried to understand what he meant.

As my cheeks burned from his gaze, I averted my eyes away from him, hoping that would calm the uncontrollable pounding of my heart in its cage. My mother's teachings echoed in my ears—*remain stoic, unemotional*. I schooled my expression into one of cool indifference.

"Is something wrong?" Brontes inquired, head tilting.

"Nothing's wrong," I replied, turning away to resume my dusting.

"Ah, yes," Brontes scoffed. "The perfect, emotionless princess. How could I forget? I shouldn't be surprised. Typical of your kind, I suppose. You are just as my parents described Ice Enchanted—stiff and detached."

A spark of anger ignited within me, but I refused to let it show. My duster continued its methodical path along the shelves, my face a mask of indifference.

Brontes prowled closer. "You think you're so superior, don't you?" he continued, his voice growing more aggressive. "Your icy powers have made you an empty, frozen shell."

I clenched my jaw, my hands gripping the feather duster tightly. My parents taught me well—emotions were a weakness, and I couldn't afford to show any. I would not give him the satisfaction of a reaction. Let the prince hurl himself against my walls. He would not find a way in.

"Tell me, Princess," Brontes sneered, as if he was trying to bait me into a reaction. "Do you ever tire of being so . . . cold? So utterly lifeless?"

His words cut through me like a knife as I battled to keep my face impassive. Though my heart screamed for me to defend myself, my upbringing silenced it. I let out a slow, controlled breath, trying to dispel the roiling emotions within me.

"Look at me when I'm speaking to you!" Brontes barked, stopping directly behind me.

My head snapped toward him with cold eyes, but my pulse quickened. His handsome features twisted into a cruel sneer. The thoughts of him being a violent monster stung my brain like a swarm of angry hornets. His own mother said he could hurt or kill me.

My heart raced in my chest as I stumbled back, unsure whether to run or stay and face his wrath. But despite all of this, something about him made me want to stay—something dangerous and alluring that pulsed beneath his skin like electricity. It pulled me toward him even as all logic screamed at me to flee.

Silence fell. His presence filled the room, as heavy and crackling as an oncoming storm. His gaze felt like a weight, pressing down in an effort to make me fold. I refused to look away or give any indication of weakness—no matter how much he tried to rattle me, I stood my ground and met his stare with quiet defiance.

"What use are you, anyway? A shadow in the background, devoid of any real substance. Perhaps you're more suited to serving as a mere decoration."

He circled me slowly, like a predator stalking its prey, and my pulse quickened in response.

"Are you just some robot my mother purchased to tidy up after the rest of the staff?" He bent forward ominously, eyes blazing like hot embers. "Or perhaps a plaything for my own entertainment?" His gargantuan frame cast a dark shadow over me, looming like a sinister mountain ready to crush me beneath its weight.

A plaything? How dare he speak to me this way!

My icy exterior struggled to hold back the torrent of emotions that threatened to spill over. The heat of his anger and challenge to my resolve only made my frigid façade harder to break. I was determined not to yield nor show him the vulnerability that he desired.

"Nothing?" he challenged, stepping closer to me. "Do you even care about anything at all?"

My mother's lessons echoed through my mind, *Remain calm, show no weakness, never let them see your true feelings.*

"Of course I do, Your Highness," I finally responded, still maintaining his piercing gaze. "I simply prefer to keep my emotions . . . contained."

"Contained?" Brontes laughed bitterly. "That's an understatement. I've seen glaciers with more warmth than you, *Princess*."

"Perhaps it's better that way. Emotions can be dangerous." As hard as I tried to remain calm, a tinge of annoyance seeped into my voice. "I do not see how my demeanor is any concern of yours, *Your Highness*."

"Isn't it?" he shot back, his eyes narrowing dangerously. "You're to be my wife, yet you act as if you're made of stone."

His words stung, but I couldn't let him know. As the raging fire of his frustration burned brighter, I refused to give into his determination to break me.

"Nothing else to say for yourself?" he taunted, his voice cold and cutting. "Fine. Just go back to your dusting. You're clearly incapable of any real conversation."

His dismissal felt like a slap in the face, but I swallowed the resentment and frustration, returning to my task. As I moved to dust another shelf, Brontes stomped over to the fireplace, his frustration evident in every step.

"You're devoid of any warmth or life. It's infuriating!" he bellowed furiously. "How does anyone expect me to marry a soulless statue?!"

My body stiffened at the sound of his roar echoing throughout the library, and I flinched as he kicked an innocent log into the fire. The fireplace hissed and popped as the flames conjured ominous shadows upon the walls. My face burned with anger, and suddenly, the floodgates finally broke.

I lifted my chin and locked eyes with him. "Better soulless than a monster."

The words were out before I could stop them. Brontes jerked back as though struck. All at once, the stormy rage in his eyes dimmed, and a mysterious expression flickered across his face that looked like the dark cloud that hung over us.

In the silence that followed my accusation, Brontes' eyes searched mine as if looking for something in them. I faltered, confused and alarmed by his sudden change in demeanor.

"Is that what you think I am?" he grumbled, his voice barely more than a whisper, but the intensity behind it was unmistakable. "A monster?"

"Isn't that what everyone says?" My voice trembled, but I held my ground, staring him down with all the courage I could muster.

He took a step toward me, and I instinctively backed away, suddenly aware of just how close we were. His expression darkened with a blazing fury that sent shivers down my spine.

"Fine!" he growled. "If that is how you truly see me, then there is nothing left to say."

With that, Brontes stormed out of the library with the book clutched tightly in his hand. The door slammed shut behind him, quaking through the walls as if the Storm Castle were trembling in response to his anger.

Frozen in the spot where our confrontation had taken place, the weight of my words settled on me like a thick fog, suffocating any semblance of satisfaction I'd momentarily felt for standing up to the prince. I called him a monster.

Monster.

The word echoed in my mind, and I questioned whether it was justified or if I had allowed anger to cloud my judgment. What had I done? I sank into the nearest chair, my legs suddenly too weak to support me, and clutched its carved arms. My chest felt hollow, echoing with confusion and dismay.

Despite his rage and barbed words, there was still something about him that I couldn't quite put my finger on—something that made me question his fearsome reputation.

Why did his anger evaporate so quickly? And why did seeing that change in his eyes leave me feeling gutted? No matter how many times I replayed the scene over and over in my mind, I didn't understand. I was never meant to understand.

I pressed my fingers to my temples in frustration. If only I were better at reading expressions, at understanding the subtle nuances of body language. But how could I be, when my entire life had been spent learning to suppress my own emotions?

A strong gust of wind rattled against the windows of the library, and the scent of oncoming rain clung to the air. Perhaps it was a reminder of Brontes' turbulent nature. What stormy emotions were swirling inside him now after I called him a monster?

The word slipped from my lips like a dagger. The instant it was out, I knew I'd cut deeper than intended. And yet, I couldn't quite comprehend why it made him so upset. Surely, it wasn't the first time he'd been called that.

Clasping my hands together, I tried to focus on the sensation of my fingers pressing into one another, grounding myself in the present moment. But the look on Brontes' face before he stormed away refused to fade. As the storm clouds above threatened to unleash their fury upon the kingdom, I realized that he was even more of a mystery to me now than he'd ever been. And it would take more than a heated exchange of words to unravel the enigma that was the Storm Prince.

With a groan, I buried my face in my hands. Mother had warned me again and again not to let my emotions show. Now I saw the wisdom in her words. If I hadn't lashed out, if I had kept my feelings contained as I was bred to do, I wouldn't be sitting here now, pulse racing and thoughts in turmoil.

Why did I suddenly feel like the monster?

CHAPTER FOUR

The following day, I was applying a fresh coat of lemon oil to the antique cabinets and display tables that lined the hallways, polishing each one until the wood caught the sunlight coming through the tall windows and glowed with an amber shine. The lemon oil had a light, refreshing scent—a bit tart and citrusy. Both clean and crisp with just a hint of sweetness.

Just as I thought about how calming the aroma was as it filled my nostrils, a deafening crash echoed through the air. It reverberated off every wall and shook the very floorboards beneath my feet, leaving me rooted to the spot in fear.

Then came the blood-curdling howl, raging through the halls like a wild beast in pain. It sounded almost animalistic.

Almost.

The voice was filled with so much anguish that it pierced my soul and forced me to move. I immediately sprinted down the winding passageways, dodging vases and suits of armor along the way, desperate to find the source.

My feet pounded against the stone floor but slowed once I reached the hallway . . . *his* hallway. The pained roars came from inside the Storm Prince's room. As I crept up to the closed door, I could discern what he was saying.

"Why?! Why does this always—" The prince bellowed.

A crash.

"Every! Time! Why can't I—"

Yet another crash.

"I try *so* hard! So hard! WHY DOES THIS KEEP HAPPENING?!"

The words devolved into a howl of hideous shouting, smashing, and destruction from inside the room. If it weren't for the words I'd just heard, I would have thought a quad-eyed yeti was locked inside there.

The whirlwind of carnage continued for minutes on end while I stood staring at the closed door, positively agape. My imagination was running wild about what the inside of the room may have looked like after the chaos subsided, when I accidentally leaned against the door, and it swung open.

I barely got a chance to glance around the room before the Storm Prince looked at me with a twisted, frightening expression. His sharp navy eyes were those of a wild animal.

"Have you come to see the monster?!" He snarled.

"I—" I couldn't answer nor explain my presence.

"Get out or I will show you a monster!"

I stood frozen in the doorway.

"*GET OUUUUUUTT!*" He suddenly turned around, then seized a clock from his bedside table. As he turned around, those crazy eyes once again fixed on me.

Then, his expression changed to one I still couldn't read—different, softer. The Storm Prince spun around and flung the beautiful clock into the wall, shattering it into a million pieces of gold, springs, cogs, and wood.

He looked back to me—that animalistic frenzy was still there, but it was somehow tempered. Brontes then stormed over and slammed the door in my face.

Oddly enough, even though the queen had warned me he was dangerous, I never felt like I was in danger, even if his belongings were. When he yelled at me in the library and now when he looked as if he might throw the clock at me, I knew he wouldn't hurt me. I knew it deep in my bones.

But I still did what he said, running around in the Storm Castle until I found someone—Rori.

"Rori," I said. "The Storm Prince is . . . destroying his room?"

It sounded like a question as I stated it, yet Rori, with her usual attitude, rolled her eyes and sighed.

"Fine. We will need all the hands we can get to replace his room again."

She began walking toward the servants' quarters, and I trotted by her heels.

"What do you mean by 'replace his room'?" I asked.

"The prince, that horrible monster, wrecks his room perhaps once, maybe twice a month."

I was getting used to expressing myself, and I let my eyes widen when I heard that.

"That often?"

"Yes," Rori replied. "So we almost always have new shipments of furniture arriving bimonthly in one of the buildings by the stables. Rumor has it they converted an old stable into space for the furniture."

I didn't know what to say to that, and we continued down to the stables.

Soon enough, I was carrying a small bedside table alongside a veritable army of staff. Half of them carried different pieces of furniture, while the other half was empty-handed. A bed, a wardrobe, a chest of drawers, a desk—all of them high-quality, well-crafted pieces.

The prince's hallway was quiet now. A head staff member knocked on the door, and Brontes opened it up. He had that same look in his eyes I recognized so strongly. His eyes moved over us all, yet when he settled on me, his eyes softened even more in a look of what I could only interpret as abject shame.

He then stepped back from the door and allowed the staff to enter. The empty-handed half walked into the Storm Prince's room and began retrieving broken pieces of furniture and other debris. I leaned my head inside the room and finally saw what the remainder of it looked like.

It was as if a beast had been let loose—the wardrobe was almost folded in half by a deep crack that spread across its center. The dark blue curtains were ripped to shreds. The pillows, duvet, and other bedding were also torn to pieces, soft insides scattered throughout the entire room. The bed stood lopsided, and the bed slats were all splintered, many of them marked with very clear footprints.

I scanned around the room as the other staff came in, working as coordinated and well-rehearsed as a military exercise as they swept up the debris, cleared away the bulk of the furniture, and finally brought out the broken pieces.

For a fleeting moment, the room was completely desolate, and Brontes covered his face, rubbing it with both hands. He gave a large, helpless sigh that overwhelmed me. I wanted to reach out to him, but I did not know what words could offer comfort to the Storm Prince.

Then, it was our turn, and I watched the other staff walk into the room and carefully lay all the replacement furniture where the old ones were. However, I realized that I didn't have a clue where the bedside table went—right or left. As the other staff moved with precision, I hovered awkwardly while I fumbled with the table's mounting weight. It felt like it was growing heavier and heavier in my hands.

A rough touch brushed my arm, sending a delightful tingle up it. The sensation instantly spread across the rest of my body until it engulfed every fiber of my being, giving me goosebumps and tightening my nipples. I knew it was Brontes standing beside me. What other man could make an Ice Princess shiver?

As I turned, my heart leaped at the sight of him standing so close to me. Then just as quickly, my chest squeezed tight with apprehension. I didn't know what to expect, didn't know how to brace myself for whatever was to come.

His gaze searched me once more. I stared up at him, willing my expression to remain impassive. If nothing else, I could cling to the habits of a lifetime. I could stay detached. I could—

"Princess, let me take that." He lifted the table from my hands as if it were nothing more than a piece of paper.

I licked my parched lips hungrily as I watched the rigid muscles in his arms stiffen with tension like steel cables, desperate to draw the energy radiating off of him into myself. His navy-blue eyes sparkled as they met mine, and his lips curled into a smirk when he saw my stunned expression.

"I don't understand why my mother is making a princess move furniture." He shook his head, placing the end table down gently on the floor. "But don't worry. I won't tell her if you won't."

"Oh," I said, taken aback that he spoke in such a kind manner, considering he had just screamed in my face not an hour earlier. "Thank you, Your Highness."

As the Storm Prince repositioned the bedside table, I realized we were alone. The others had completed their tasks and left me behind.

Brontes' demeanor was so different than it was an hour ago or even earlier in the library that it caught me off-guard for a moment—not just his tone but by everything I hadn't seen before in him. Warmth radiated from his skin. Light danced through his black hair, like lightning rippling through a dark thundercloud, as strands of it fell over his peach-toned face, and how he looked at me with a sparkle in those deep, navy-blue eyes in a way no one else ever had.

"Your Highness, are you okay?" I asked him gently.

He looked up at me, eyes wide in surprise. "What?"

"You seemed like you were in a lot of pain earlier," I replied.

Suddenly, the Storm Prince stepped back from me. "Princess, I—" He stopped mid-sentence, clenching his jaw. The muscles in his neck tensed, and I could feel the storm inside him brewing once more.

"Your Highness?" I tried to catch his gaze, but he kept his eyes fixed on the ground, his fists clenched at his sides.

For a long moment, he stayed deep in thought as if struggling to decide what to say and how much to say.

"I'm fine," he finally mumbled.

"Are you sure?" I pressed.

"I'm fine, dammit." A hard look passed over his eyes, his expression transforming back into the one I had seen in the library. "Leave me," he grumbled, his voice straining with the effort of keeping his emotions in check. "Please, just go."

"Your Highness, I—" My voice faltered, my resolve crumbling under the weight of his intensity.

"Go!" he roared, his eyes flashing dangerously as they met mine.

As dangerous as his eyes looked, I knew they were just acting as a shield. So I nodded at him and started to leave.

"Princess?" he said.

"Yes?" I paused, looking back at the Storm Prince.

His expression had softened, a hint of vulnerability behind his hard stare. "Thank you for asking," he said quietly.

My breath caught in my throat. For a moment, I wondered if I should stay. Maybe I could pull aside his veil of anger and get to the heart of what was bothering him. But I knew that wasn't my place—at least not yet—so I simply nodded and left, closing the door quietly behind me.

Though obviously our engagement was arranged, I couldn't deny the magnetic pull from him, drawing me closer whenever he was near. Watching the way his muscles flexed sent a warmth that spread through my body. His eyes—dark and intense yet filled with an undeniable warmth when he first looked at me. His touch—gentle yet electric, even if only for a fleeting moment. Could these small glimpses be signs of who he truly was beneath that rough exterior?

A multitude of questions weighed heavily on my mind as I walked away. What turmoil raged within Brontes? What demons were consuming him? Were they stemming from his past or something more recent? Had he been trying to say something else before he clammed up and sent me away?

When I arrived back at the servants' quarters, they were all grumbling about how cleaning up the prince's room again had cut into either their break time or their chore time, but for once, I avoided them and sat on my own bed to think about what had made Brontes so upset.

"I wish the king or queen would slap some sense into that monster," Rori snapped to Dagur. "How many more times are we expected to clean up after his tantrums?"

Dagur chuckled. "At least that monster isn't throwing the furniture at us!"

As I listened to them talk about the Storm Prince as they usually did, I couldn't help but feel a twinge of sympathy for him. They were all so much better at recognizing facial expressions than me—how did they not see his pain?

Maybe he'd hidden it so well until that point . . .

My heart hurt to see him—anyone, actually—in so much pain. I didn't know why I could see it while the others couldn't. Maybe it was because I knew what it felt like to be trapped in a castle, surrounded by people yet completely alone.

Fannar was the person I needed when I felt so alone. If I was the only person who could see Brontes' pain, then it was up to me to be that person for him.

CHAPTER FIVE

"Not bad," the queen snapped at me contemptuously. "It appears that you are not completely dreadful at the art of the fan!" she declared. "Let's see how good our wretched ice girl is with the tea ceremony."

I was told that I needed to understand Storm powers and how they worked—including giving me a number of lessons on how to protect myself should there be a raging storm inside the castle walls. The moment I realized she was teaching me this in case I was caught in the middle of one of Brontes' outbursts, I felt like the picture was becoming a little clearer. She didn't teach me anything on how to speak to or even act around my new fiancé—only how to ignore and escape him.

Tucked within these lessons were a number of ordinary etiquette techniques, so amongst my teachings of how to duck and avoid a storm inside the walls were methods on how to be a lady. During my time at the Storm Castle, I had started to become proficient at them all.

The queen loudly clapped her hands twice, and three servants bowed and left the room. They returned with a tray and several different pieces of equipment in their hands: two huge ornate porcelain bowls, a jar, a teapot, and four cups.

"Pay attention, girl," she ordered. "We have a very particular way of preparing our tea here. We use the lightning in the bottle to roast the tea leaves in the first bowl, then use the clouds to summon fresh, clear water to mix it. After that, you must use more lightning to boil the water and control the winds to stir the tea."

I waited for her to demonstrate, but she merely pushed the jar toward me. Inside the glass, I could see a tiny storm crackling and whirling away.

When I continued to wait for a demonstration, she tutted and gestured toward it. "Go on, stupid girl! We don't have all day!"

After I gestured to speak, she nodded impatiently at me.

"Your Majesty, how do I draw out the storm?"

"Well, that is what makes this your most challenging task yet."

She folded her arms and stared down at me with those hard eyes. I didn't think it was *quite* disapproval or disdain, but it was close.

So I hung my head over the jar. "Okay . . ." I looked at the wild thing, fighting itself inside its glass prison. As I looked at it, I was a little afraid at first—the tiny storm curling and twisting, wrenching itself apart and forcing itself back together. Yet as I stared at the storm, it occurred to me how *small* it was and yet how vicious it had become, simply because its prison was smaller.

If it had more space to move, I figured, *then it wouldn't be tearing itself apart like that.*

Once the thought occurred to me, it wouldn't leave me. With bolstered bravery, I took hold of the jar's top and pulled it open, letting the entire storm out.

"Wait!" The queen yelped as the storm spilled out of the jar.

However, just as I thought, as soon as the storm was free, it ceased to be one storm viciously eating itself. Instead, it split into three separate clouds that drifted apart—one cloud striking lightning, one starting to dribble with rain, and finally, a little tornado spinning away from the table.

I stood on the table to catch them as they floated toward the ceiling, gently reaching with a cupped hand and easing the clouds back down toward the table. I pulled the lightning cloud over the bowl of tea leaves, then the rain cloud over an empty bowl. Finally, after making my way to the corner of the room where the tornado cloud had gotten stuck, I easily coaxed it back to the table with gentle hands.

The queen was staring at me, eyes wide, mouth agape, but she said nothing, so I just kept on with my task.

I tapped the little cloud grumbling with thunder, and with my encouragement, a small bolt of lightning struck, hitting the tea leaves in the bowl and causing them to shrivel and brown. I turned my attention to the empty bowl, and the hovering rain cloud began to fill it with water. Once the bowl was filled, I gently pushed the rain cloud back into its jar. After easing the rumbling thunder cloud over to the water bowl, I tapped it a few more times, allowing lightning to hit the water and boil it. Scooping some of the roasted tea leaves into the boiling water, I gingerly wrangled the baby tornado into the bowl, which swirled the leaves around. Soon, between the lightning strikes and the whirling of the tornado, the hot water turned into a light brown tea.

"Incredible . . ." The queen murmured as I carefully replaced the two remaining clouds back in their jar. As soon as I did, the three clouds merged again into a fury of chaos.

I poured the contents of the tea into the teapot and left it to brew. "Is this acceptable, Your Majesty?"

The queen was shaking her head lightly. "You were not supposed to *let the storm out!* Do you have *any* idea how dangerous that could have been?!"

I could not keep her gaze, but I found the strength to answer from somewhere within. "I knew it wasn't going to be dangerous. It was only ripping itself apart because it didn't have the space to grow."

I expected a smack, a simple *Do not speak back to me!* yet I got nothing in response from her. I looked up at her again in time for her to give a *humph.*

"Well, for future notice, that's not how we perform the tea ceremony. You're supposed to reach into the jar and draw the sections of the cloud out piece by piece."

"Wouldn't the lightning burn my fingers, Your Majesty?"

Her face curdled at me—becoming what I now recognized as a sneer. "The women of the Storm Kingdom have dealt with it for centuries. Do not question our traditions, horrid ice girl."

I looked back down after that. "Yes, Your Majesty."

After that, she picked up the teapot and poured a cup from it.

"Let's see if your reckless ways have at least produced a worthwhile cup of tea."

She put the cup to her lips and took a taste. She got a strange expression on her face—it looked like more rage somehow, until her lips twisted, and she snapped. "Ugh! It's not terrible." The queen poured two more cups, then placed them on the tray. "Bring these two cups to the king and the prince upstairs. The prince should be in a lesson, and I would imagine a relaxing cup of tea would be exactly what they need."

"Yes, Your Majesty."

"Next time," she snapped. "I expect you to brew the tea properly, but this is acceptable to bring up to them for now."

She placed the tray in my hands. I bowed my head, then walked out of the room. As I approached the king's study, I was a little excited. I knew where it was from cleaning the hallways, but I'd never been allowed inside before.

My excitement soon tapered when I heard shouting coming from inside the room. The door was open, and I was privy to all of it.

The prince wouldn't destroy his father's study. That wouldn't make sense. I cautiously poked my head around the corner of the door. The tray of teacups shook lightly in my hands as I watched in horror as the king held Brontes by the throat. The Storm Prince teetered on the tips of his toes under the grip of his father.

"How did I end up with a son as embarrassing as you?!" the king snarled in Brontes' face before throwing him against the wall.

Brontes slammed into the wall with a loud crash, then fell over but kept silent.

"Did I raise you to be so *weak?*" The king continued. "Has all this time mentoring you been a total waste of my time? *Well?!*"

Brontes was on the floor for a moment, just trying to draw in a breath, but a steely tone in his eyes gleamed before he turned around, still on the ground. "You taught me to be loyal to the Storm Kingdom, and I am," Brontes spoke. "I don't care what you say—those fine people signed up to protect our kingdom, and I am *not* throwing their lives away!"

As the Storm Prince struggled quickly to his feet, the king marched toward him, snarling, "They agreed to live by the sword, and they know they will die by it—some sooner than later. You act like an idealist, but you're a fucking coward. That is what *you* are!"

As the king drew close, Brontes flinched away from his father, refusing to look him in the eyes, and turned his face away—but he still spoke with defiance. "There has to be another way than using an entire company as bait! A faux retreat, followed by a flank—decoy knights, *something!* We haven't even established communications with the other kingdoms to attempt talks of peace yet!"

The king's eyes narrowed. He spoke oh, so quietly. "Are you insulting my experience?"

"Father, no, I—"

The king's hand snapped out and struck Brontes across the face with a teeth-grinding *smack.* The impact rattled so loudly through the air that I flinched when I heard it. Brontes didn't react that time, only looked to the floor and pressed his hand to his reddening cheek.

The king spoke more softly than ever, almost whispering. "You think you know better than me when it comes to war? You think we can just send a few letters back and forth between the other kingdoms and war would be averted? You think it's that damn simple?!"

Brontes didn't answer. He only stared at his father.

"The kingdom will be destroyed under your govern if you're too pathetic to make decisions like this. I am *ashamed* to call you my son."

Brontes stood, his hand clenched into a fist by his side, flashes of lightning sparking around it.

When the king noticed the sparks, he stepped back with his eyes slightly wider.

Huh? Is that . . . fear?

I wasn't quite sure, but either way, the king snapped at him. "You're dismissed for the day! Get out of my sight before I *really* hurt you!"

Brontes bowed slightly at his father, gritting his teeth. "Thank you, *Your Majesty.*"

He turned, storming toward the door.

I'd completely forgotten that I wasn't invisible, that I was physically standing in the doorway. Brontes' eyes were fixed on the floor, but as he reached me, blocking his way, something feral flashed in his eyes. Instantly, his hand smashed the tray out of my hands.

I yelped as scalding liquid skimmed over my hands and arms. The metal tray clattered as it hit the marble floor, like a cymbal crashing to a halt. The teacups and saucers clinked against each other, bouncing off the floor before shattering, and rattled as they came to a rest in countless porcelain shards. Their contents spread over the floor in a dark puddle as the hot tea pooled outward. The pungent aroma of burnt leaves lingered in the air.

My cry reached Brontes in a way the other sounds hadn't. He blinked and came back to himself. Then he met my eye. Looked at the mess he'd made.

"Oh, gods." He murmured quietly in his realization.

Then there was that pain in his eye again. He returned his gaze to me, and I saw that same tender look. I met his eyes—I had to show him I wasn't afraid.

As I stood in shock, the hot liquid seeped through my dress, making the fabric cling to my body and wetting my skin with its warmth.

He looked like he wanted to say something—he even opened his mouth—then his eyes flickered to his father. He turned and sidled past me politely, making sure not to touch me or step on anything as he did.

Just before he left, he stole one more gaze at me. Deep, sad eyes. I met his gaze, still trying to show him I wasn't scared—wasn't judging him. As he stared back at me, there was another change in there. Something softer.

But then he left. He had to.

I couldn't help but stare after him as he left, but then the king gave a *humph*. Then he said his first words to me, "Are you lame, girl? Clean that up!"

"Y-yes, Your Majesty!"

I dropped to my knees and cleared the mess as quickly as I could—but not quickly enough to find Brontes after I was done. He was gone.

CHAPTER SIX

"Why do you want to know more about the prince?" Maisol asked, frowning at me. "You've been here long enough. What more is there to know?"

As Maisol and I were making desserts, the kitchen was filled with the warm, sweet smell of cookies baking in the oven. Vanilla, nutmeg, and cinnamon wafted through the air, sweet and delicious, with a hint of melted butter and brown sugar.

"It's just . . . he's going to be my husband someday, so I should know more about him, that's all."

Maisol whipped cake batter. "Can you crack three eggs into that bowl?"

Moving to an adjacent counter, I did as she asked while she continued, "He's been the same way since I've worked here. I don't know what else to tell you."

"Would anyone know?" I asked, bringing the bowl over to her.

Maisol peered into it, then shook her head with a sad smile. "Gwyn, there are eggshells in there. You have to pick those out."

"Oh, sorry." As I dipped my fingers into the bowl, the slimy consistency made my skin crawl, so I concentrated my focus on Maisol instead.

"You're the one getting private lessons from the queen," she said. "Hasn't she told you anything about him?"

"Only that he's dangerous and could hurt me." I washed my hands and re-presented the bowl of eggs to Maisol, who began to beat them with a hand whisk.

"Yes, that's what we've been told too." Maisol nodded. "We've all been instructed to keep our interactions with him as brief as possible. I mean, you've seen what he does to his room. Fetch the basket of black cherries. You can start deseeding them now."

I nodded and retrieved the fruit and a small knife.

"Actually," Maisol perked up. "Nana Osborne's been here forever, so she might know more about your prince."

"Oh, really? Where is she?"

"I think I saw her polishing silverware at the servants' table."

"Do you still need help, or can I . . . ?"

Maisol rolled her eyes at me. "Go."

The old woman sat by herself inside the food storage room at the massive wooden table that served as the communal dining room for all the servants, polishing silverware.

She smiled at me, deep wrinkles on her face lifting in the gesture. She removed her gigantic, thick-rimmed glasses and wiped the lenses with her apron before placing them back on, as if to get a better look at me.

"So, you want to know about the prince, do you?" She winked at me.

"Yes, please, Nana," I replied eagerly as I picked up a polishing cloth and spoon to help.

"Well, when he was a boy, he was bright, cheerful. I was his primary nanny from the time he was four until he turned twelve. He spent his entire childhood running around the castle—the library, the courtyards, the gardens . . ." Her hands glided over a butter knife with a polishing cloth. "Since he didn't have any playmates, he learned to play alone, and he had such a wonderful imagination." She gave a fond laugh. "He kept me on my toes, let me tell you!"

"When did he start to change?" I asked curiously.

Nana Osborne sank down in her seat as I placed another polished spoon into the silverware box. Her brows furrowed, and her aged lips saddened. She picked up a fork from the pile and began wiping it. "Well, I suppose as he grew older, he started to become more aware of what people thought of him—as all children do—and he became more desperate for his parents' approval. I think the problem was that the queen has always been . . . difficult to work for, so servants were hired and fired, like a revolving door of staff, and that left poor Brontes with no one, really. Every time he found someone to look up to, they'd cleaned the stables wrong and were gone a week later. His parents weren't *there* in his life so much, but I suppose they were *present.*"

"I see."

"At the age of thirteen, both the king and queen took more of an interest in his life, probably realizing they needed to prepare him to become king one day. I don't know what they did to that poor, sweet boy I knew, but the next time I saw him, he was a completely twisted version of my Brontes . . . and then it only got worse." Nana shook her head, pain reflected on her face.

I wasn't sure what came over me, but I placed my hand over hers. "The queen told me that he almost killed someone. What happened?"

Nana Osbourne nodded, her face somber, and her voice sank with emotion. "It was the day his powers manifested," she said, her eyes far away. "He was only sixteen, so no one expected him to manifest for two more years. Many of us were in the courtyard with the king and queen when he stormed over to them. I knew something was wrong when I saw his face." She shook her head sadly.

I could see the memories playing out in her mind—Nana Osborne reliving that fateful day.

"He had this look of rage—a seething anger I'd never seen before on him," Nana continued. "He was furious at them. I don't know why, but you know how teenagers and their parents can be. They frequently argued, but this time it was different."

She took a deep breath before continuing her story. "The king and queen argued with him for a few minutes. The prince screamed at them and then . . . suddenly an explosion of lightning flew from his hand, hitting one of the gardeners who had been standing nearby." She closed her eyes in sorrow at the memory.

"It was terrible," Nana sighed softly. "That poor gardener nearly died that day. The queen was so enraged that she had the prince locked away for weeks." Nana shook her head sadly as tears brimmed in her eyes.

I gasped. "But why? Wouldn't she want to help him control his powers?"

"No, she wanted him to show restraint and obedience, nothing more. She thought it would teach him how to be a better ruler one day, but it only made things worse. The king and queen immediately banned the use of powers in court, believing they posed too much danger."

She shook her head slowly, her lips pursed in a tight line of sadness. "And Brontes . . . Brontes never recovered from what he had done. It was obviously an accident. No one could have known that his powers had manifested, not even Brontes himself! But it changed him forever. He became more withdrawn and isolated himself within the castle walls, refusing to open up to anyone since then. Even me."

Her gaze fell to the floor as she sighed heavily. "It's a shame, really. He used to be such a loving boy, always smiling and laughing, but now . . ." Nana let her voice trail off before continuing her work on the silverware.

"The entire royal family became more and more unbearable after that day." She shook her head again, some disdain entering her expression. "Much of the staff abandoned the castle, and they were right to."

I was speechless for a moment, wringing my hands in my lap, before finally finding my voice again. "Do you think that boy you used to know is still in there?"

Nana Osborne didn't answer right away. She gave me a knowing look and a wide smile. "I think so, if you really wanted to find him. I've seen signs of the Brontes I knew." Her eyes were soft behind her thick glasses as she gazed at me. "Perhaps a kind fiancée might be exactly what he needs, if you're willing to try."

I nodded, and Nana Osborne patted me on the shoulder.

"Knock-knock!" Maisol said as she entered the room, carrying a plate of freshly baked cookies. "How was she, Nana? Was she helpful?"

"Oh, yes, very much so!" Nana replied.

"That's great!" Maisol replied. "Did she stab herself at all?"

"Not once!"

Maisol chuckled. "Better than having her in the kitchen then! The princess can't handle a potato peeler without cutting herself somehow!"

They both laughed. I could tell it was well-natured, but my cheeks still flushed with heat.

Maisol turned to me. "Your beloved Storm Prince has requested a mid-day snack. Since you're asking so many damn questions about him, we've decided you've drawn the short straw, Gwyneira." She handed me the cookies. "Go take these to his study."

The plate of cookies warmed my hand as I knocked on the ajar door to the Storm Prince's study.

"It's open," A sullen voice called from the inside.

The prince's study was slightly smaller than the king's but just as grand. Luxurious emerald-green rugs covered the marble floors. The rough stonework walls were elaborately adorned with tapestries, paintings, and ancient scrolls.

Rich velvet chairs clustered in pairs, and bookshelves brimming with tomes lined the walls. Dotted between them were various intricate wood and marble carvings depicting storms and heroes that lived once-upon-a-time. A large map table sat in the center of the room underneath a beautiful chandelier.

Natural sunlight filtered through sky-high windows, filling the entire room with warmth. The only sounds in the room were the steady ticking of an old grandfather clock and Brontes' pencil scratching against paper as he furiously wrote at his desk.

He didn't look up as I made my way into the study. "If that's the snack I requested, put it on the map table."

"Yes, Your Highness," I replied, walking over to the map table and placing the plate of cookies down onto it.

Upon hearing my voice, his head whipped up. "Princess?"

"Yes, Your Highness?"

Brontes slowly got up from his chair and walked toward me.

"No need to stop what you're doing," I urged. "I know you're busy. I just wanted to bring the cookies to you."

"No, it's okay. I need a break." Brontes stared at me for a long moment, his gaze intense as always but this time laced with sadness.

"Are you okay, Your Highness?" I asked with concern.

He broke eye contact and reached over the table toward the plate of cookies. "I'm fine," he said quietly, picking up a cookie. "Thank you for the snack. I appreciate it."

"My pleasure," I replied, trying to be cheerful, but I could tell he wasn't fine.

The Storm Prince chewed the cookie slowly, staring at nothing on the map table, and the room fell silent again.

Suddenly, I remembered the altercation he'd had with his father earlier and, without a second thought, blurted out, "What you did earlier was very noble."

He looked up and gave a dry laugh. "Noble? I smacked boiling tea out of your hands! I could have hurt you."

I was surprised that's where his thoughts were, even after having time to mull it all over. "No, I meant with the military meeting with your father. It's very noble you weren't willing to sacrifice those men and tried to work toward peace by talking to the other kingdoms instead."

"Oh." He sounded a little surprised and then shrugged a little. "I just said what I thought." He took another bite from the cookie.

"Yes, but to the face of the king," I replied firmly. "That was brave. I know I couldn't have done that."

His eyebrows raised, and his eyes softened. "Thank you."

I tried to think of the perfect words to say next to the prince, but so many questions swirled around in my mind. How did he feel about me? What could I do to make him happy? To bring back the boy that Nana Osbourne knew? But fear held me back. The words got stuck in my throat like a chunk of dry bread, and before I knew it, my body turned to leave on its own accord.

"Princess?"

My breath caught with excitement as I turned around.

"I owe you an apology," he said quietly.

I shrugged. "It's okay. It was just tea."

"No." He shook his head. "In the library, I said things that I didn't mean, and I shouldn't have. It was out of line, and I'm sorry." He paused, jaw tightening. "I'm not great at controlling my temper, so sometimes my anger just . . ." He trailed off, but my heart ached so much that I hardly noticed. I still grappled with the vulnerability he was suddenly showing me, and my attempt to find words to convey how I felt came up empty.

His dark navy eyes searched my face, waiting for my response, but when none came, he looked away. "I get it. I know you never wanted to be here. I'm sorry for making it worse."

As he turned to go back to his desk, panic surged within me. The thought of continuing this conversation made my stomach lurch, but I didn't want this moment to end, not yet. I didn't want him walking away thinking I felt nothing.

"Wait," I said softly.

He froze, his wide gaze snapping back to mine.

It's okay to be vulnerable. I reminded myself with a deep breath. *Speak honestly.*

"I-I don't hate you," I finally said.

"What?" He frowned lightly.

I couldn't continue without breaking his intense gaze. My eyes studied one of the ornate rugs on the floor as I spoke. "When we first met, you said that we hate each other. Well, I don't know if you hate *me*, but I-I don't hate you."

The Storm Prince's brows furrowed, and he stood silent for a moment. "You looked like you hated me when I tried to talk to you in the library." His statement hung cold in the air.

"I-I didn't mean to . . ." My voice shook, but I pushed on. "I have a hard time . . . showing emotion." I rubbed my own arms in a loose hug. "And I don't know how to read other people's emotions well. It's . . . not something that we did at home. So I'm sorry that I didn't respond the way you expected me to or if I came across as unemotional."

I paused, my heart pounding in my chest as I finally looked up at him to face his reaction. He watched me with an unreadable expression, but I didn't see a sign of anger.

"I will try harder," I continued earnestly. "To be more open with everyone . . . but especially with you."

He was silent for a moment before nodding slowly. "I understand," he said quietly. "I'm a monster."

"No!" This time, I looked him firmly in the eyes. "I'm sorry that I called you that. I was just mad."

"You were right, though. I can be a monster."

"I don't think you're a monster." I took a step toward him. "I want to understand you. The light, the darkness, and all the things in between."

A smile curved on his lips at my words, and as his powerful gaze lingered on me, excitement fluttered in my stomach. The prince took a step closer to me until his breath tickled my neck. My heart was pounding in my chest as his hand came up to brush a stray strand of hair behind my ear. The touch was gentle, yet it spread warmth through me like wildfire.

"And I want to understand you, Princess," he said. "If you'll let me."

I smiled shyly at him. "Yes, I'll let you."

CHAPTER SEVEN

As Maisol pulled the ribbons of my corset tight across my back, my back arched into an uncomfortable position.

"No, Gwyneira!" She laughed. "Stand straight! It won't choke you if you just keep still."

"Why are we doing this?" I asked, looking down at the massive black and royal-blue hooped skirt. "Am I getting married already?"

"No, why would—" Maisol started, then paused and restarted. "No, you're right. The queen would absolutely plan the whole wedding and tell you about it last." She gave another sad chuckle, then continued. "But no. You're just here to eat dinner with the family."

"Why does that require three hours of preparation?" I sighed, a little frustration slipping past me.

After lunch service, several of the queen's handmaids collected me from the kitchen. Since then, I'd been stripped, shoved into a perfumed bath, scrubbed head to toe, and aggressively dried off before being dressed in brand-new undergarments. The women dragged me to a boudoir, where they painted my nails, styled my long white hair, and bombarded my face with powders and paints.

Eventually, my hair was done up in a tight updo and pinned with wires adorned with glittering gold jewels. My appearance was painted to fit in with the darkened environment—smoky eyes, dark lips, and black fingernails, which I thought were an odd choice.

Finally, Maisol came in with an apologetic smile and a very, *very* large dress. Since then, we'd been wrestling with the corset.

Maisol undid the ribbons and began lacing it up again. While she did that, she answered me. "To be honest, I don't know why it takes so long, but I've heard that the male servants have had to do the same over the Storm Prince for years, so it's not just you."

"Really?"

I thought about Brontes and his moodiness. What an ordeal it must have been for everyone involved.

"But why?" I asked. "Why does everyone need to be so fluffed and puffed up for a single dinner?"

Maisol pulled the ribbons tight—I gasped in surprise—but the corset finally seemed tied properly.

"There we go," Maisol murmured. "Should be okay now."

She patted my back twice and moved in front of me, still focused on the dress.

"They've always been the type to try to woo other kingdom royalty with fancy dinners."

She looked up at me with a cocked eyebrow.

"I believe that's how they got your parents to agree to the betrothal. A fancy dinner with Brontes dressed up like a handsome doll on his best behavior. I'm sure that's what they're planning with you too—dress you up like a little doll and show you off at parties to show off how well the alliance between the Storm and Ice Kingdoms is going." She cackled a little. "Then once they're gone, they just stick you back in the servants' quarters like putting fancy dishes back in the cupboard!"

That was when someone poked their head in. "Is she ready? The queen grows impatient."

Maisol and I took one last look in the mirror. My dress was a deep, dark red with lace and velvet trim. It fit tightly around my waist and flared out into a long train that trailed behind me as I walked. The bodice was dotted with pearls and crystals that glimmered in the light of the chandelier above us. On my feet, I wore black velvet slippers lined with gold threading; around my neck hung a large black onyx necklace set in gold. Dark colors weren't popular in the Ice Kingdom, but they were beginning to grow on me here.

Maisol nodded at my reflection in the mirror. "Yes. She's ready."

I walked with an expert posture, hands linked gracefully in front of me. The hooped skirts were difficult to walk in without tripping, but I managed it as my escort led me into the dining hall. When she swung open the doors, I felt myself both frozen in terror and gaping at its opulence. It was almost like the throne room, except for the table that stretched the entire length of the room. It had very dark walls, with slim windows barely letting any light in.

On this gigantic table, the king and queen sat at the far end, so far away that I couldn't read their expressions.

The prince sat halfway down the table, far away from his parents. He looked utterly miserable.

"The Princess of the Ice Kingdom, Your Majesty," my escort announced.

"Your Majesties. Your Highness." I curtsied at the king and queen, then at Brontes.

The queen nodded. "Sit her next to the prince."

The servant then led me forward and gestured to the chair next to Brontes. As we drew closer, Brontes only looked at me from the corner of his eye.

I sat down next to him, and Brontes looked back to the table in front of him. I wasn't sure what to say to him, but then he spoke first.

"You look beautiful, Princess."

He said it so quietly, but I felt myself flush a little when he did. Out of the corner of my vision, I noticed his smile as he caught sight of my blush.

"Thank you, Your Highness," I whispered.

"Right," the queen said. "Now that we are all here, let us practice."

She clapped her hands, and the doors on either side of the table opened, and a small army of servants wheeled dishes in. Bowls of steaming soup were placed in front of us. I looked at Brontes, who was looking at his parents.

Then the king picked up his spoon, followed by the queen. I watched Brontes pick up his cutlery—and the queen smacked her fist onto the table. "Do not pick up your cutlery before her, you imbecile! You two eat *together!*"

"Sorry, Mother," Brontes said quickly.

"The King eats first! Then the Queen! *Then* the Prince and Princess!"

"Sorry," Brontes repeated.

The Storm Prince looked over to me, his eyebrows creasing worriedly. I gave him a small smile. Brontes returned it with a half-smile, then hovered his hand over his spoon. I mirrored his movements exactly, and his half-smile spread into a full one. He drifted his hand left, then right. I followed it perfectly. Brontes snorted a little in laughter under his breath. Then we picked up the spoons at once and finally started eating.

That was when the queen slammed her fist on the table a second time. I tensed up in response, and Brontes bristled next to me. She jabbed a finger at me. "Elbows off the table, you ghastly girl!"

I realized I'd leaned forward a little and sat up straighter. Finally, I started eating. It was extremely uncomfortable. I could feel the queen's gaze burning into me, and my throat was getting so tight in my discomfort that I could barely swallow. Soon, I put down the spoon, my soup half finished. When I did, Brontes quickly noticed and put his own down too.

I realized I'd just stopped him from finishing his soup, but the staff, ready and waiting, swooped in and scooped up the bowls from our table before I could say anything. I did what I could to mouth *Sorry!* to him, but Brontes just gave that chuckle again.

As they took the soup from us, the king spoke. "So, Brontes," he said, "Tell me about the economic weaknesses in the Earth Kingdom and how such a thing could be taken advantage of in the case of war."

Immediately, the Storm Prince's mood changed. I could almost see the sweat building on Bronte's brow, and he shuffled in his seat, clearing his throat.

Across the table, the king's eyes narrowed. "We covered it only a few days ago."

Brontes nodded.

When he started listing out the reasons, it sounded so well-practiced, monotone. Sitting so close to him, I could see the light dimming in his eyes as he droned on. It was so horrible, my chest tightened as I watched the life drain from him. But as the second course was placed in front of us, Brontes finished his answer, and the king nodded approvingly.

Then the king picked up his fork to eat. Then the queen. Brontes looked at me and slowly raised a hand. I mirrored his motions, and he started snickering. I couldn't help but start laughing under my breath as well.

"What is so funny?" The queen snapped.

"Nothing, Mother," Brontes answered quickly.

He met my eye, and we both started to eat. This time, despite how little appetite I had, I continued to hold my cutlery until Brontes had finished eating. We were in complete silence, but Brontes gave me a grateful smile anyway.

The second plate was swiftly picked up by staff, but as they did, my cutlery rolled off my plate and began tumbling down.

Out of instinct, my hand snapped down to catch it. Brontes did the same.

My fingers clasp the end of the fork, and Brontes caught the other end—then gave a sharp cry of pain.

"Do not pick up the cutlery from the dirty floor. That is what the staff is for!" The queen snapped at me first before frowning at Brontes. "What happened?"

"Nothing. Just . . ." Brontes was rubbing his fingers together. "It's just cold."

"*Cold?!*"

She had been yelling at us the entire time, but I knew this was particularly bad because her voice got very low, and her eyes sharpened. She stood up, leaning over the table and glaring at me.

"I'm not hurt, Mother. It's not—" Brontes started, but she cut him off.

"You vile piece of trash!" The queen jabbed a sharp-tipped finger in my direction. "I told you to *never* use your powers here! And you would do as much the *first* time you have the privilege of being allowed to eat with us?"

"I-I'm sorry, Your Majesty!" I squeaked out. "I didn't mean too."

"Are you mocking the Storm Kingdom?! You Ice Enchanted always think you're better than us. Do you understand the *depths* of your disrespect?"

"No! I promise I'm not! It was an accident!" I insisted.

"Mother—" Brontes tried again.

"*Guards!*" she snapped.

Suddenly, I was surrounded by armor-clad knights.

"Take this *cursed* girl away and give her thirty lashings for her disrespect!"

Suddenly, the entire table shuddered underneath us all. My head snapped over, and Brontes smashed both his fists onto the table hard enough to knock every single person's glass over. He stood, glaring at the queen.

"*Enough!*" he snarled.

Brontes turned around and stabbed a finger at the guards around me. "You're not taking her *anywhere!*" He then turned back to his mother. "That was a mistake, and you know it! That's *not* fair!" The strong presence that emanated from Brontes in that moment washed over me. Sparks of lightning scattered around his fists, but it was *nothing* compared to the sheer *power* that radiated from him.

But the queen's face curdled into a snarl. "You do *not* talk to me like that, you fool!"

"She was not being disrespectful, and you know it!" Brontes roared. "Don't change the subject!"

"We do not allow magic to be used in the courts! No exceptions!"

"She is a *princess* from a *foreign* kingdom. Of course we make an exception for that!" Brontes countered.

"This is not up for debate! She broke the rules and must pay the price. Either that damn Ice Enchanted gets thirty lashings . . ." The queen folded her arms and pinned down Brontes with her stare. "Or you get *fifty!*"

I shuddered, staring at Brontes in shock.

He delivered his own fearsome gaze at his mother before firmly saying, "I'll take the fifty."

"Fine!" The queen grunted, then glared at the guards and nodded.

The guards then stepped forward and took him by the arms. He continued to defiantly stare down his mother.

"No!" I protested.

"Take this insufferable girl away too! Put her back in the servants' quarters where she *clearly* belongs! I knew bringing miserable Ice filth into my home would be a mistake."

CHAPTER EIGHT

The moment the guards released me into the servants' quarters, all the female staff members were gathered around, gawping at me.

"Oh, my gods!" Maisol said. "What happened? The servers said there was so much shouting!"

"Did the prince do something?" Rori asked.

"Come on, tell us what happened! We need details!"

But I didn't have time for them. Instead, I tore the fancy dress off my body. As I did, I looked at Maisol. "If anyone comes looking for me, can you send them away?"

Perhaps my sudden undressing dumbfounded them, but once I was free from the burden of my gown, I pulled on my servant's uniform and sprinted toward the door.

"Thank you, everyone! I promise I'll tell you everything later!"

Then I turned and dashed away.

I knew it was a foolish idea, but I made a beeline for Brontes' room. I was scared of what was happening to him—the torture he hadn't hesitated to take off my hands.

A servant girl waited outside his room. She was wearing a bonnet and an apron and carried a large bowl of lightly steaming water with lengths of bandages slung over one arm.

I was about to say something to her when a large *CRACK* rang through the corridor, followed by a long, raspy grunt. The girl opposite me cringed visibly, her eyes squeezing shut.

"How many lashings is that?" I asked softly.

"I counted about thirty-eight," the girl whispered back.

Another *CRACK*.

"I can take that if you want," I said quietly.

She looked up at me, eyes wide.

"You'd do that for me?"

"Absolutely. Just . . . can I have your bonnet and apron?"

She nodded at me, then put the bowl down to untie her apron. "You'll probably need it for the blood," she said as she handed both her apron and hat to me and wasted no time in leaving.

The next eleven lashings rang out as I tied the apron around my waist and donned the bonnet, pulling it far down over my head so it covered my face. Sometimes

Brontes would grunt or shout between blows. Sometimes he remained silent.

Soon, the armored guards left Brontes' room, a somber look on both their faces. "You may go in to tend his wounds now."

The knight barely looked at me—just as well, or they might have recognized me from the dinner. But they, too, left very quickly.

As I entered Brontes' room, he sat on the bed with his back facing me. His hands were rooted deep in his black hair, but that wasn't what drew my eyes. His massive back had been split open, and blood dribbled all the way down to his bed.

My heart felt like it was being torn in two. "Oh, my gods . . ."

Brontes flinched and looked over his shoulder. "Princess? What are you doing here?"

His wounds appeared worse as I walked closer, looking more painful and bloody with each step.

"I was worried about you, Your Highness." My voice swelled with concern as I sat behind him on the bed.

"I'm fine," he grunted.

I dipped the cloth into the warm water and started to wipe the blood off his back. I very carefully wiped the spaces between the strikes, clearing the thick smears of scarlet from his skin. Brontes stiffened when I touched him, but he didn't say a word.

"Why did you do that?" I asked softly.

"Do what?" Brontes asked.

"Take the punishment in my place. You didn't have to do that."

He just shook his head. "It wasn't fair to you . . . Plus, I'm used to it."

The bowl of water turned bright pink as I swirled the cloth inside. With more of the blood wiped away, my breath hitched at the spider web of long-healed scars that visibly crisscrossed the entire length of his back. *How many times have his parents put him through this? And for no reason at all?* My heart ached.

"Don't cry," Brontes said lightly.

I realized I was indeed crying and wiped my eyes. "Sorry, it's just . . ."

"It's okay," Brontes repeated.

"It's *not* okay!" I insisted. "I thought *my* parents were bad, but—" When I realized I was speaking badly of the king and queen, I bit my tongue.

Yet Brontes started laughing lightly, his warm back shuddering under my palm. Then he looked over his shoulder, smiling at me. "I'm glad I'm not the only one who thinks that. Everyone else acts like this is normal."

"It's not normal," I said firmly. "Why does she do this?"

He shrugged under my hand. "It's about control. It's just how she is. I guess I can't blame her . . ." He trailed off, shuffling a little underneath my hand, and then said quietly, "Since I can't control myself. You've seen what happens when I get angry. I destroy things. I'll keep going and going until my knuckles are scraped down to the bone, and yet . . ." Brontes leaned over, grabbing his own hair in his fingers. "I don't stop. I'm hurting *myself*, and I can't stop." He sighed loudly. "I guess if it weren't for my parents, I probably would've hurt someone again or even killed someone by now."

He slowly looked over his shoulder at me again and sounded like he was lightly choking on his words. "If we got married and I—"

"You wouldn't hurt me." I stared into his big, sad blue eyes. "I know you wouldn't."

Not saying anything in return, he looked away as if he didn't believe me.

After wiping all the blood from his scarred back, I put the towel down to examine his wounds once more to ensure they were thoroughly cleaned. I'd felt Brontes' warmth before but never this close with so much of his skin exposed. Ice Enchanted had a lower body temperature to match our freezing environment. His warmth mesmerized me, and I couldn't help but touch him. As my fingers traced one of his rugged scars, his body heat seeped through my fingertips and spread over me.

"Oh, my gods!" He jumped.

"Sorry!" I yelped. "Did I hurt you? I'm so sorry!"

"No! You're *cold!*" He laughed. "Your hands were just in hot water! How are you still so cold?"

"I don't know." His laugh lifted some of the weight off my heart, despite what had just happened to him. I glanced down at my pale hands, the water droplets freezing onto the surface of my skin.

Suddenly, his tan hands reached forward and grasped mine.

"Wow," he said. "Ice cold . . ."

Warmth coursed through my body again at his touch. Tense energy radiated off him like static on a piece of fabric, and I expected to be shocked at any moment. The power ebbed and flowed within him, waiting to erupt.

"Gwyneira," he said softly, still lightly holding my hands. "Can I call you Gwyneira?"

My heart soared at hearing my name leave his lips for the first time. "Of course, Your Highness," I replied, almost breathless.

"Call me Brontes." He gave me a half smile. "You probably ought to, considering everything."

"Well, Brontes." I smiled back. "I still need to put your bandages on. Stop squirming, or I'll freeze you on purpose!"

As I wrapped bandages around his broad back and muscular chest, Brontes asked, "How long have you had your powers?"

"Actually, I only got my powers when I arrived here, the day after . . . Well, you know."

"The day you got kidnapped."

Hearing it phrased like that took me aback. My hands stopped moving.

"Isn't that what happened?" he asked defiantly. "You were dragged away from your home into a strange land and forced into a betrothal with a man you never wanted to marry." He glared at the floor with his thick eyebrows furrowed. "It's disgusting what they did to you. I'm sorry. If I could send you home tomorrow, I would. Hell, I think about running away from here all the time, and it's my home . . . but I owe it to the Storm Kingdom to be a better king than my father. I just have to survive until then." Brontes turned his head toward me. "And I'll free you as soon as I can. I'm so sorry, Gwyneira."

He shook his head and fell into silent despair after he spoke. After I tucked in the end of the last of his bandages,

I ran my hand over his back—partly to comfort him, but mostly because I wanted to touch him again.

"I'm actually happier here than at home," I said softly.

"Really? How is that possible?" Brontes whirled around completely to face me fully, eyes wide. "What was your life like *before* that this is an *improvement?!*"

It was my turn to stare at the floor as I spoke. "My parents were never very nurturing, so after my brother was born and they had an heir, they didn't intend to have more children. I was a mistake in every way possible. They made that abundantly clear. Fannar—" The sadness from mentioning his name caused my breath to hitch for a moment. Brontes cupped my hand in both of his with a sympathetic look in his eye.

"They made sure Fannar received an education and proper training since he's the future king. I lived in a tower of the castle and was forbidden to go anywhere else. I spent nearly every moment of my entire life in just a couple of rooms. There were a few handmaids that brought my meals, and my brother came to see me every once in a while, but otherwise, I was so alone . . ."

I smiled lightly, looking at Brontes again. "But here, I have friends to talk to, to laugh with. The queen may scold or slap me every now and then, but I can go anywhere in the castle. When I go back to the servants' quarters every night, I get to walk underneath the stars outside. In the Ice Castle, I could only see them from the other side of a window. Life is good here."

In spite of my enthusiasm, Brontes still looked sad and gently shook his head.

"What's wrong?" I asked.

Brontes' sapphire eyes, soft with compassion, lingered on me for several moments before he leaned in, and his powerful arms drew me into a comforting embrace. His impenetrable chest enveloped me in a safe cocoon, like a fortress meant to protect me from the despair of my past.

"Life *isn't* good here, Gwyneira," he said softly, pulling me in closer.

I allowed myself to sink into his chest and listened to the reassuring beat of his heart beneath the bandages that were wrapped around him. *He smells so good.* When I closed my eyes, I lost myself in his grounding scent, like the smell of cedarwood after a fresh rain shower.

"I promise I will show you what a good life is meant to be."

I didn't know if there was anything left to say, so I just let myself feel. My cheek flushed as it melted into his unexpectedly soft bare skin. My fingertips glided over his bandaged chest, and a delicious heat filled me. I snuggled into his arms.

CHAPTER NINE

Chaos ripped through the air with a deep roar and a cacophony of smashing objects, shattering glass, twisting metal, and snapping wood. Rage echoed off the walls, reverberating through the room in an unending roar of destruction.

A few weeks had passed when Maisol and I walked by the hallway that led to Brontes' room—and heard the familiar sound of destruction. After the night he took my punishment, Brontes had been noticeably warmer toward me. I even tried to convince the other servants that he was not an uncontrollable monster, but they wouldn't believe otherwise. This was certainly not helping my case.

"Ugh," Maisol groaned, rolling her eyes.

Brontes. My heart sank.

"That monster is destroying his room again," she continued and turned around to go back the way we came. "C'mon. We need to let everyone know so we replace his room *again.*"

"Um . . ." I murmured. "You go ahead. I'm going to check on him."

She scowled for a moment, then shrugged. "Suit yourself, but you still have to help us."

As she walked in the opposite direction, I dashed into Brontes' room, where the floor was littered with items that had been crumpled like paper under his strength. It was just as bad as the last time he destroyed it. I looked at him. His face twisted in pain. His fist was stuck through the front of the wardrobe.

"Brontes!" I exclaimed. "What's wrong?"

He ripped his fist from the wardrobe. His eyes ran wild, and he sucked his breath in through gritted teeth. "*Get out of here, Gwyneira!*"

"Brontes, what's happening?"

"*Get out!*" He screamed and then took a few deep breaths before adding, "I don't want you to see me this way."

I didn't get out. I just got closer.

"Brontes, what's going on? Please, tell me!"

He covered his face and gave an incoherent roar.

I lightly placed a hand on his arm. As soon as I touched him, a sharp shock jolted through me, causing me to gasp and stumble back in surprise. His veins pulsed and throbbed with a power so wild and untamed that it threatened to break free at any second. His body struggled to cage the monster within him.

Or the storm within him . . . Suddenly, it clicked.

I ran my hand up and down his arm. "Why don't we take a walk outside?"

"What?" Brontes crossed his arms, gripping his own biceps as if he was trying to keep his body from falling apart. "I can't leave. I'll hurt someone out there . . . or worse."

"You won't," I said with confidence.

"How do you know?" His navy eyes looked at me with deep-rooted terror.

I placed my hand on his cheek. His aura crackled with energy against my palm. "We'll go to that big empty field on the side of the castle, okay? No one else will be there." I pulled him toward the door. "Come on."

When we got outside, Brontes seemed to calm down a little bit—that or he was just doing a better job at cramming down his feelings. He still had his arms wrapped around himself like he was physically trying to hold himself together.

But I was confident.

The starry sky looked like deep black velvet scattered with diamonds, sparkling away. The Storm Castle was now a distant silhouette in the evening light.

"Oh, how *beautiful!*" I gasped enthusiastically.

Brontes didn't look up, instead clutching his chest like he had severe heartburn.

"Those stars are so sparkly—but maybe . . ." I took a deep breath and tried to find that zone of concentration I needed when I practiced my powers in the servant's quarters. Once my mind calmed, a rush of cold power coursed through my veins.

I met Brontes' gaze before I threw my hand forward. Bright white ice scattered across the ground in an askew pattern.

Brontes gasped. I did it again, except this time, I concentrated even harder until I shaped the ice into a five-pointed star.

"Yay! I did it!" I cheered in joy.

His eyes darted back at the castle. "If my parents catch us doing this, they're going to kill both of us!"

"Don't worry," I assured him. "I'll ask my friends to cover for us."

Brontes blinked at me anxiously. I touched his arm again. The power inside him still raged.

My mind skipped to the storm in the jar, so violent in its containment yet so peaceful when it was released. The queen said that releasing it wasn't the way things were done, but how could they not know that bottling up a storm was a horrible idea?

"When was the last time you used your powers, Brontes?"

He shook his head. "I don't remember."

"Why don't you give it a try? I think it might make you feel better."

Brontes looked at his hands, and they sparked as he stared down at them. "I've never tried. I break things *without* my powers . . ."

"There's nothing to break here," I assured him. "It's a clear sky, a wide space. Give it a try."

He looked at me, gave me a sad smile, and chuckled. "I don't even know how."

I took a few steps back and gave him an encouraging smile.

Brontes brought both his hands forward, fingers arched. Sparks crackled around his palms.

He closed his eyes, and the pain and the anger on his face came right back.

His hands flared so brightly that I couldn't look at them. Brontes opened his eyes, then leaned, a little scared, away from his own hands.

"Up there! Into the sky!" I chirped.

He glanced at me. Then, with a monstrous roar, he thrust both hands into the sky.

CRACK! Lightning split the sky, the thunder bellowing across the heavens as the electricity flew away into the ether.

I cheered, clapping my hands.

Brontes was panting hard when it was over. I started to walk over—when he did it again, thrusting his palm out, more lightning cracking forward.

More lightning. More. The more powers he used, the more black grumbling clouds gathered overhead.

He started screaming incoherently as he threw lightning, and as the rain started tumbling down from the sky, it became even more impossible to hear what he was saying.

Eventually, he seemed to tire himself out. He then slumped, panting, arm braced on his knees.

That was when I decided it was safe to come over and see him.

"Are you okay?" I asked him.

When I put a hand on his shoulder, the frenzy under his skin calmed.

Brontes stood up, still panting, and smiled softly at me. "Yes, I . . . actually feel *better*." He said it like he couldn't believe it. "I had no idea using our powers would . . . do that." He looked up at me. "How did you know it would work?"

I shrugged. "I saw a storm trapped in a jar before, and the little cloud tore itself to shreds. Let it out, and it was perfectly peaceful."

Brontes frowned thoughtfully. "Why aren't you scared of me, Gwyneira? How do you know I won't hurt you? You said so yourself. Everyone else thinks I'm a monster."

"I'm not everyone else." I blinked at him, slightly offended. "I'm your future wife."

He paused as his face lit up with a huge grin. "Indeed, you are."

He didn't say anything for a while, so I looked up at the rain still pouring down on us. I concentrated hard and then waved my hands through the air, finally attempting the feat I'd never dared to try before. The rain suddenly shifted, turning into snow as it fell. It quickly began layering the grounds, turning the field white.

"Wow," Brontes said appreciatively. "This place looks so different covered in snow!"

"It looks like my home," I answered breathlessly.

Brontes leaned down and started drawing his fingers through the snow. "I've never seen snow before."

"Really?" I gasped. "How?"

"It's always warm here. Warm and humid."

He stood up and walked around in a circle, listening to the light crunching under his boots, looking around at his footsteps, and laughing in childish joy.

I'd never seen someone see snow for the first time. I'd never seen someone's eyes light up when they saw something that I saw every day.

I got a wicked idea and started scooping up the snow into my palms. Once I'd balled it up in my hands, I shouted. "Brontes!"

He looked up at me, and I flung the snowball at him. It hit him right in the face and burst outward into powdery snow. Brontes gave a shriek, then swept an arm across his face. But then he gave me a wicked grin and leaned down to sweep up a handful of snow himself. He caught onto the concept of a snowball fight extremely fast, and soon, we were flinging snowballs back and forth, dodging side to side as we launched frozen projectiles at each other.

One of my snowballs hit his chin, and the ice fell down his neck. He yelped as wet snow dripped down into his clothing, trying to shake it out. I laughed and started to run.

"Oh, no!" He laughed playfully. "You get back here!"

Suddenly, the air around me turns into a blustery breeze. It swept me off my feet and carried me back to Brontes.

I looked at him—he had his hand extended, controlling the wind. In his other, a snowball.

"No! Brontes, no, no, no!" I shrieked with laughter.

The mini tornado carried me over to him, and when I got there, he caught me around the waist. He crumbled the snowball above my head, aiming to drop it into my collar. I kicked my legs, squealing as the snow fell down the back of my neck.

"You can't be that cold!" Brontes teased. "You're from the Ice Kingdom!"

"It's still *cold!*" I insisted.

As we both laughed, his eyes sparkled with amusement, and his firm arms dipped me gracefully, just like a couple at the end of an elegant dance.

The cool snowflakes kissed my flushed cheeks as they drifted down from the inky night sky, coating the secluded field in a blanket of white powder that stretched for several yards in every direction. The world seemed to hold its breath as snow danced through the air, soft and unhurried, intertwining with one another before settling gently on the ground.

A sudden gust of wind blew my long white hair across my face and billowed my dress around me. I brushed the strands aside and looked at Brontes, who watched me with an expression of admiration tinged with something else that I couldn't quite put my finger on.

His large, warm hand steadied my back while the other swept stray locks of hair away from my face. My heart fluttered as his fingers lightly caressed my cheek.

"You are so beautiful," he murmured. "So perfect."

His stunning words caused my breath to quicken. His stormy eyes glowed with an intensity that made my knees weak.

How is this happening?

"But I'm cold," he added playfully, a mischievous smile tugging at the corners of his lips.

I laughed.

"My turn." He raised a hand toward the sky.

The falling snow melted in mid-air as Brontes willed the temperature to rise. Within moments, droplets of a gentle rain shower cascaded down upon us.

The water warmed my chilly skin, causing goosebumps to ripple across my flesh. I tipped my head back, closing my eyes and smiling as the rain streamed over my face. The only sound was the patter of raindrops against the earth that synchronized with the beating of my heart. We might have been the only two souls left in the world.

As Brontes pulled me closer, the fervor of his strong arms wrapped around me, pressing our rain-soaked bodies together, was intoxicating. His fingertips traced along my spine, making me acutely aware of the damp fabric clinging to my skin. My nipples twinged with each touch, our connection electric and undeniable.

The water droplets clung to his dark lashes, making his stormy eyes seem even more alluring. His wet hair, usually unruly, now hung in loose, damp waves that framed his chiseled face perfectly. The rain trickled down his soaked shirt, and the fabric clung to his muscular chest, leaving little to the imagination as it accentuated every sculpted curve and contour. Brontes had always been handsome, but now he looked utterly breathtaking, like a force of nature in human form.

Maybe it's because he's a Storm Enchanted, but I've never seen him look more gorgeous than in the rain.

Brontes gently wiped some of the water off my face. He paused to carefully brush away the droplets that had frozen to my cheeks like tiny diamonds. Yearning for his touch to linger on my skin, I grasped his hand and cradled its warmth against my cheek. My fingers ran over his rough knuckles and calluses.

"Gwyneira." His deep, husky voice sent a shiver down my spine that had nothing to do with the temperature.

His gaze locked onto mine, a smoldering intensity burning within them that made me catch my breath. For the first time, I felt appreciated and wanted by someone. I wasn't a mistake or a burden. I was desired. And that realization filled my heart with a warmth that no fire could ever match. At that moment, something within me shifted forever, and I knew there would be no going back from whatever this was between us.

As if in slow motion, Brontes leaned closer, inch by inch, until I could feel the warmth of his breath. My breath hitched in thrilling anticipation. I parted my lips as my heart pounded in my chest. I'd never wanted anything as much as I wanted his kiss. Those beautiful dark blue eyes never left mine, watching, waiting, savoring this exquisite torture he caught me in.

When at last his lips met mine, I melted into him. The tenderness of his kiss surprised me, like the brush of a butterfly's wing against my skin, a soft, slow, gentle caress that set my blood on fire. My heart took flight.

As we kissed, Brontes' strong arms tightened around me, pulling me closer as if he never wanted to let me go. I pressed myself against him, my body molding to his, feeling every contour of his muscular form.

The world around us faded away, leaving only the sound of the rain and our own heartbeats to penetrate the haze of emotion that enveloped us. Time seemed to stand still.

He pulled back slightly, his eyes searching mine for any hint of doubt or uncertainty. But all he found was the reflection of his own desire and adoration shining back at him.

"Is this real?" I whispered softly in disbelief.

"Very real." Brontes' cheek nuzzled against mine.

Our bodies pressed closer together, driven by an undeniable need for connection. My hands grasped the wet fabric of his clothes, feeling the strength of his muscles beneath them, and my own body responded in kind, arching toward him, seeking solace in his embrace. My arms found their way around his neck, fingers tangling in his damp hair, pulling him impossibly closer.

As our lips met once more, I thought back to the countless hours I'd spent alone in my tower, reading about love and longing for a connection of my own. Those stories fueled my dreams, filling my heart with an ache for something I had never truly experienced.

Now, as I tasted Brontes' sweet lips and felt the steady thump of his heart against my chest, I realized that those tales paled in comparison to the indescribable magic of kissing him in the rain.

The moment was more perfect than any I could have ever imagined, more spellbinding than any words that could ever be written.

Those dreams of romance were now a reality. *My reality.*

CHAPTER TEN

"I don't know what you did to him!" Rori laughed one evening as I washed dishes in the kitchen with Maisol. "But the prince has been much more manageable since that night you snuck out!"

Dagur laughed hard as well. "Maybe we should let you sneak out more often!"

The change in Brontes was dramatic after that night I'd taken him down to the field and encouraged him to use his powers. The night we'd . . .

He'd stopped destroying his room. He was a lot more polite to everyone, including the servants. He seemed generally happier and more relaxed than I had ever seen him. The Storm Castle suddenly had a lot more random, unpredictable thunderstorms, but no one really cared. After all, it was the Storm Kingdom—thunderstorms weren't uncommon at the best of times.

I never told them about him using his powers or even the kiss, but our growing relationship . . . well, that was a little harder to hide.

The mere mention of him would cause my cheeks to flush, and the teasing would begin. Brontes asked for me far more often, and even when he didn't, any order which came from the king or queen to do something for Brontes would be passed from servant to servant until it reached me.

After Brontes protected me from the queen's wrath at that dinner, she called me an evil witch who'd cast a spell on her beloved son and forbade us from spending time alone together. So the other servants kept my visits with Brontes a secret, despite the fact that I was merely fulfilling my duties when I saw him.

"It's definitely been easier to deal with the prince since you've been around," Maisol agreed. "Even if you can barely do your chores!" She laughed.

I shrugged. "I think he just needed a little compassion and to try something different. That's all."

Maisol gave a little grunt and kept scrubbing at some grease on a plate. "You sound like Nana. I don't think any of us would have been able to help him."

I chuckled lightly.

The kitchen door opened behind us, and one of the housekeepers called in, "The queen insists the prince's study is too dusty for her son to concentrate!"

Maisol smirked at me. "Speak of the devil."

My eyes lit up at the thought of seeing Brontes.

"Go on!" she encouraged. "Get out of here!"

The housekeeper swapped places with me and started washing the dishes in my stead. I took the feather duster and furniture polish from her, then happily made my way to Brontes' study.

I walked into his study, shutting the door behind me. Brontes looked up from his desk and smiled. I loved how instantly his eyes lit up and a wide grin spread across his face whenever he realized it was me and not another servant.

"Gwyneira! What are you doing here?" He jumped from his chair and closed the gap between us in a few long strides.

Before I could answer, he embraced me in his thick, muscular arms and pressed his lips against mine.

"Apparently, your study is so dusty that you can't concentrate." I leaned back to twirl the duster in the air.

"Mother *was* trailing her finger along the shelves and groaning before she left." He chuckled lightly and then frowned at his desk. "I wish I could just hold you all day, but I need to finish my work before Father returns."

I nodded, and Brontes returned to his desk. He quietly pulled the velvet curtains aside to welcome in more sunlight through the large windows, illuminating the room with a warm glow. A handful of silvery dust particles danced in the air as the feather duster glided along one of the bookshelves. It wasn't nearly as dusty as the queen made it sound, but knowing her high standards, I meticulously swept every surface, careful not to allow any speck of dust to escape my sight.

Brontes scribbled on some papers with that look of misery in his eyes.

"What are you working on?" I asked.

"A stupid impromptu test on military tactics from my father." He rolled his eyes. "I hate it, especially since I don't agree with the way he does things."

"Wait, you're the future king. Why aren't you attending the academy, like Fannar?" I asked curiously. "Did you already graduate?"

"No, I'm only three years older than you!" He chuckled.

"I thought the Enchanted Council requires all future rulers to graduate before they could ascend the throne. At least that's what Fannar told me."

Brontes sighed. "My parents insisted that I be taught in the Storm Kingdom. They harassed the Council so much that the Council granted an exception for me." He shook his head in disdain. "I would have loved to attend the academy, like your brother, and meet people from other kingdoms."

"Yeah, me too," I said wistfully. "I always thought I would join Fannar in the fall. He'll be a third-year by then. I would've been a first-year, so I don't think we'd have many classes together, but I always imagined we would study together."

Tears prickled the corners of my eyes as I thought about Fannar and how much I missed him. The room felt heavy with my sadness, and I sighed deeply, wishing I could see him again.

I remembered the letter I'd written to him before coming to the Storm Castle, begging him to come and rescue me. I realized now how silly that was. Two kings and two queens had arranged my betrothal. The politics behind it were beyond me, beyond Fannar, and even beyond Brontes.

But a part of me had been convinced that Fannar would kick down the door to the Storm Castle within the first week of my arrival. After all, he'd always managed to find his way into my tower to give me books and gifts, even when our parents locked the doors and banned him from seeing me for long periods of time. He was my big brother, and it felt like he could do anything.

"Oh, Gwyneira . . ." Brontes rose from his chair and pulled me tightly into his broad chest. "You're really close to him, huh?"

I gave a slight nod as my reply, not wanting to say anything more, or I might break down.

"You'll see him again," he promised. "I'll make sure of it." Brontes was silent for a moment and then said, "Tell me a *happy* memory about him."

My mind immediately drifted back to the stars. "Remember how I told you that when I was in the tower, I wasn't allowed outside, but I could see the stars from my window?" I began. "I always thought they were so *beautiful,* so endless, so free . . . like they were their own little worlds above our heads."

I smirked with fondness and a little embarrassment as the memory came back to me. "Then Fannar told me that there *were* other worlds up there—different planets—and that some of the stars shining down weren't stars at all but other nearby planets. Since then, I've always wanted to know everything about them!"

Brontes nodded, amused by my enthusiasm.

"Then, when Fannar's powers appeared . . ." I laughed. "He would sneak into the tower and sculpt me my own play observatory!"

"A *play* observatory?"

"Yes! It had a big ice orrery in the center, ice telescopes, and planetary models. None of it was real, of course, but I used to play in that little ice observatory for hours! When Fannar came back, I'd tell him of all the imaginary new planets I'd 'discovered' with the ice telescopes that didn't even work!"

I wiped a tear of laughter from my eye with a sigh. "As I got older, he started bringing me astronomy books from the castle library or bought them for me whenever he stumbled across one our library didn't have. Oh, speaking of the academy, up until the time I came here, he'd been trying to find a book for me at their library that I've always wanted to read. They have one copy, but he told me that it's always checked out."

"What's it called?"

"*For the Love of Stars: A Study of the Cosmos,*" I said the title as if it were a lovely daydream. "Hopefully, one day, I'll get my hands on it!"

"I hope so too." Brontes smiled and then said quietly, "I'm sure it comes as no surprise that my parents didn't let me have many friends growing up. They didn't want me getting into any trouble or wasting my time on frivolous activities like playing with other kids. But they did buy me a really nice telescope for my eighth birthday since it was considered 'educational.' It seemed huge when I stood next to it! I used to love looking at the stars too." His eyes shined with nostalgia. "As I got older, I stopped using it. Life just got in the way." He shrugged to himself.

Hearing the sadness in him as he spoke, my hands found his, and our fingers interlaced as we stood together.

"How about we look at them together on the next clear night?" I offered with a soft smile.

"Sounds good." He squeezed my hands. "Well, Fannar sounds like a wonderful brother. I can't wait to meet him *soon*. If anything, my parents have to let him come to our wedding."

My heart fluttered with excitement at the thought of *our wedding* and having Fannar there.

"I guess you're right." I beamed and suddenly, realizing I was no longer sad. "Thank you, Brontes."

He brushed my cheek with his hand and leaned down for another kiss. This time, it was slower, sweeter, and savored for a little longer.

"Are you done with those tests yet, son?" The king's voice rattled through the door.

Brontes and I jumped apart. He went back to studying, and I went back to my dusting. Like nothing had ever happened.

CHAPTER ELEVEN

A few days later, the scent of roasted meat and warm bread still lingered in the air as I scrubbed at the stubborn remnants of dinner off a sheet pan, my fingers raw from the effort. The other servants moved around me in a choreographed dance, their laughter a welcome balm to the usual silence that permeated everywhere else in the palace.

"Did you see the look on the king's face after he spilled the gravy?" Rori giggled, and a few other girls laughed with her.

"Enough chattering," Dagur admonished gently, though I could see the ghost of a smile on his lips. "There's work to be done."

Suddenly, a large figure appeared at the kitchen entrance, his presence casting a hush over the room, and everyone began to bow. As soon as I realized it was Brontes, I immediately curtsied with the others.

"Your Highness," our acknowledgments echoed among each other.

That's odd. Why is he here? The royal family never ventured into the "lowly" kitchens. If the queen knew, she'd probably be furious with him. The other servants shared my surprise, their eyes darting at each other with worried looks on their faces.

"Please, everyone, carry on." Brontes gestured at everyone, his eyes scanning the space until they landed on me. "Ah, Princess."

"Is there something I can help you with, Your Highness?" I asked nervously.

"I'm afraid there's been a spill in my study. Would you mind cleaning it for me?"

I nodded, drying my hands on a nearby towel. "Of course, Your Highness."

My heart skipped a beat at his request. I wondered what he could have possibly spilled, but I was excited about spending time with him.

After quickly grabbing a small bucket and clean towel, I followed behind him, "After you, Your Highness."

He grinned, guiding me out of the kitchen and into the quiet halls of the palace. But I noticed he started leading us away from his study.

"Brontes, where are we going?" I asked.

He paused, turning to me with his eyes twinkling mischievously.

"Actually, Gwyneira, I have a confession." He ran his fingers through his hair smugly. "There is no spill. I just wanted to spend some time with you."

I giggled and shook my head at his admission.

"It worked, didn't it?" Brontes turned to me with a grin. "Remember, you promised that we'd look at the stars together. Want to take a walk in the gardens?"

"I'd love that." I nodded, unable to shake my silly smile.

He took the bucket and towel from my hands and placed them underneath a table that lined the hallway. "We'll just hide these here for now." He winked at me.

We ventured outside, the night air cool and refreshing compared to the heat in the castle kitchens. The palace gardens stretched out before us like a dreamscape. I'd never seen it at night before. It was a breathtaking sight, bathed in the silver glow of the moon.

Tall hedges lined the paths, ornate fountains danced in the shadows, and flowers bloomed in vibrant bursts of color. We wandered along the stone paths, surrounded by an abundance of vibrant, fragrant blooms. The sweet scent of night-blooming jasmine delicately perfumed the air as we passed through arches covered with climbing roses.

The starry night sky stretched above us, glittering brightly in the pitch-blackness of the night. Millions of stars twinkled and glimmered like diamonds in a vast sea of darkness, adding to the surreal beauty of the moonlit gardens.

"Oh, Brontes, I've never seen so many stars," I marveled in a low whisper, fearing that I would disturb the serenity of the night.

"Neither have I." He glanced at me with a smile that made my heart race. "They must've all come out for you."

Brontes' hand found mine, fingers intertwining as if they were always meant to fit together. As he led me down a winding stone path deeper into the gardens, the distant sounds of the castle faded into the background, replaced by the rustle of leaves in the cool breeze.

"This way," he said, gently guiding me to a small pond nestled amidst a grove of flowering cherry trees, the sweet scent of their blooms filling the air. Moonlight danced on the water's surface, casting shimmering reflections onto the delicate petals overhead. The entire universe disappeared and left us standing at the pond's edge, swept away by pure, unending beauty.

"Brontes, have you ever seen anything so enchanting?" I breathed, utterly mesmerized by the scene unfolding before us.

"Only you." His eyes twinkled like the night sky, and a coy smile played on his lips. "I never knew what people meant when they said the stars were romantic, but you look gorgeous in starlight, Gwyneira."

I tilted my head to look up at Brontes standing beside me, his gorgeous tan face sparkling in the moonlight. His dark unruly hair was lightly tousled by the breeze around his sharp features. His eyes had a rare aura of peace in them.

My thoughts wandered back to when I first arrived at the Storm Castle. Brontes was so different from what I had envisioned—powerful and intimidating, yes, but also warm, loving, and infinitely more complex than I could have ever imagined.

As he stepped closer to me, heat radiated off his body. His presence alone was enough to make my heart beat faster and my breath catch in my throat. His broad and strong frame seemed larger than life, and I felt tiny in comparison—like a mouse next to an elephant, in many ways, helpless. But despite this, his closeness comforted me, as if he was constantly protecting me from some unseen evil.

"C'mon, there's more." Brontes motioned, guiding me gently toward a nearby path, his hand warm in mine, our fingers intertwined like the roots of ancient trees.

The moonlight shimmered upon the softly swaying petals of peonies as we ventured further into the garden.

"Almost there." His lips curved into a mysterious smile.

As we rounded a bend, a secluded alcove came into view. A canopy of blooming roses on a backdrop of a thick tangle of flowering vines enveloped us. A bench was nestled in the center, dappled with shadows under the pale moonlight. The scent of their perfume filled the air, creating an intimate haven that seemed to exist just for us. We sat down together, the cool stone beneath me grounding my racing thoughts, reminding me to just enjoy the present.

He gestured toward a nearby trellis where deep crimson petals unfurled under the starry sky. "The roses remind me of your cheeks when you blush."

Naturally, my pale face flushed immediately in response, and he chuckled at my embarrassment.

Brontes wrapped his arm around my shoulders, and I leaned into him, reveling in the warmth of his embrace. Our fingers intertwined under the quiet beauty of the night sky. Side by side, we gazed at the stars as our conversation flowed effortlessly.

"Look," he whispered, his breath warm against my ear. "Can you see Soxarus? He truly is a magnificent constellation."

My eyes followed his outstretched finger, locating the familiar pattern in the starry expanse above. "Yes, there he is. So bold and commanding, just like his namesake." I released an idyllic sigh. "Isn't it incredible how the stars can make one feel so insignificant yet so connected at the same time?"

"It is. Even when we were kids, we looked up at the same stars together."

Touched by the thought, I glanced at him, our eyes meeting briefly before we both turned back to the sky. Our unspoken dreams and silent confessions created an invisible thread that bonded us together.

"Gwyneira, I have something for you," Brontes said excitedly. "Close your eyes."

My curiosity piquing, I obeyed without question, anticipation building in my veins. I heard him shuffle something from under the bench and then felt something heavy land on my lap.

"Okay, open them," he said.

When I opened my eyes, my breath caught in my throat, as I gasped, "My gods . . . Is this . . .?" Resting on my lap was a book. "*For the Love of Stars: A Study of the Cosmos,*" I said in awe, my voice barely above a whisper, not wanting to wake myself in case I was dreaming. For a moment,

I sat perfectly still with my hands clasped to my chest, frightened the book might vanish if I touched it.

Brontes chucked. “It’s okay. Touch it!”

My fingertip delicately traced the title of the rare and expensive book with a reverent touch. It was etched in gold lettering on a soft black leather cover with gilded edges. It looked like it had been read multiple times, yet it was still in remarkable condition given its age. My fingers circled around a crisp light blue ribbon bookmark that stuck out of the pages.

“The bookmark reminds me of the dress you wore when we first met.” Brontes smiled.

“I can’t believe you remembered.” Tears welled up in my eyes as my fingers traced over the intricate cover again.

“How could I forget? You looked ravishing that day when I first laid eyes on you, even if I never told you.”

“I meant the book!”

Laughter bubbled up between us.

“Oh, well, your face lit up when you spoke about it,” he said. “I wanted to see that smile again.”

“How did you find it?”

“Let’s just say I have my ways.” His eyes flickered with a mischievous glint.

“How long before you have to return it?”

He shook his head. “No, silly, it’s yours.”

"Really? I can't believe you did this." I marveled at the incredible gift, touched by his thoughtfulness. "But I can't keep this in the servants' quarters. It's too precious, too valuable."

"That's okay. I'll keep it safe in my study, and you can come to read it whenever you like."

A warm smile spread across my face as I looked at the book, then back at Brontes, and I threw my arms around him. "Thank you!" My words hardly captured the depth of my gratitude.

"Anything for you, my princess." Sincerity shone in his eyes. "I just want to make you happy."

"Brontes," I murmured, turning toward him.

Time stood still as our eyes met, and my heart swelled with joy. I still couldn't believe the book I'd wanted for all these years rested on my lap. But even more unbelievable was the wonderful man beside me. The power he had over me ran much deeper than words could express or actions could display.

My lips met his in a tender, lingering kiss, the only way I knew how to convey how much he meant to me in that moment.

Brontes drew me closer to him, wrapping his rigid arms around me. I snuggled against him, laying my head on his chest to feel the strong, steady thump of his heart and breathing in his earthy scent. As I closed my eyes and sank into the solid mass of his body, never had I felt so safe. It was perfect. Being held in his arms, I knew that this was the only place where I ever wanted to be. Where I was always meant to be.

As we stared up at the constellations etched into the fabric of the universe, the canopy of roses above us seemed to glow in the moonlight, their petals casting delicate shadows on the ground. Their scent filled the air, intoxicating and sweet. That night, my love for the Storm Prince blossomed amidst the beauty and tranquility of the royal gardens under the watchful gaze of the stars.

CHAPTER TWELVE

Her Majesty was so pleased with the cleaning of Brontes' study that she requested it done on a weekly basis. The housekeeper was more than happy to trade duties with me—she would wash the dishes from lunch service while I tidied up the prince's study.

During every visit, I made sure to do a thorough job, dusting every nook and mopping every corner of the room. As I cleaned, I found myself laughing along to his anecdotes while Brontes scribbled away at this desk.

Once I finished, I'd pull my book from the hutch on his desk, curl into one of the armchairs, and open up *For the Love of Stars: A Study of the Cosmos* to the page I had left off the previous week.

Sometimes, Brontes and I sat quietly, the only sounds coming from his pencil scrawling against paper and the turn of the pages in my book. But even in the silence, just being near him made me feel alive and secure.

I kept my reading sessions brief so that I wouldn't become a burden to the other servants. I had to get back to the kitchen to do my other tasks, after all.

After a few months of this routine, I entered his study on what started off as a regular day. However, Brontes beamed with unmistakable excitement.

"Gwyneira!" He practically jumped up from his chair, gesturing wildly as he spoke, and moved twice as fast as usual. "I'm so glad you're here! I need your help with cleaning something different today."

He rushed over to the far corner of the study, nearly vibrating with happiness, and stopped in front of a door that led to the room next door. I'd seen the inside once before. It was mostly used for storage. I couldn't imagine why he needed it to be cleaned so suddenly, nor why he would be so positively giddy about having it cleaned.

"You want me to clean the storage room?" I asked. "It's filled with junk. It'll take me forever!"

"Well, you better get started then, huh?" He flung open the door with a huge grin and gestured for me to go inside. "Here it is! The disgustingly dirty storage room."

As I stepped inside, my eyes were met with a shine so bright it blinded me. Every surface in it glimmered dazzlingly with polished metal.

A magnificent copper-colored orrery was the focus of the room. Its central sphere was crafted from gleaming bronze, and the orbiting planets sparkled with rubies and sapphires. The celestial bodies spun around each other in a beautiful show. The faint ticking of the planetarium as it rotated was the only sound, other than the hitch of my breath at the glorious sight.

The exterior wall, which had already been floor-to-ceiling windows, was now lined with five telescopes of various sizes pointed toward the sky over the Storm Kingdom. A large, plush rug sprawled behind them, ready for peaceful stargazing.

Mahogany shelves of books, jars, and glass instruments lined the remaining walls in between mounted star maps and diagrams of the constellations. On top of a table flanked by two cozy lounge chairs sat an opened map and my beloved book, *For the Love of Stars: A Study of the Cosmos*.

I paused, blinking my eyes in disbelief. When the wonderful sanctuary didn't vanish, I placed my palm on top of my book as if it were the only thing keeping me on solid ground.

It *was* real. An observatory. A brand-new observatory from what I could tell.

"Brontes . . . how?" I murmured, tears beginning to fill my eyes.

He leaned against the door, arms folded, a coy smirk on his face. "What? I just decided to remodel this storage room, but the construction crew left such a mess." He ran his finger over the door frame and showed it to me. There was nothing there. "They left this place *so* dusty! And there are so many little things here that need cleaning!" He grinned at me. "I imagine that to clean this place properly you'll have to spend a couple of hours here *daily*. I'm assigning this task to you, and I'll let everyone know that you have the *extremely* important duty to clean out this filthy storage room. *Understand*, Princess?"

"Yes, Your Highness." I nodded as tears streaked down my face.

Brontes came over and ran his hand up my arm in a slow caress with a worried look. "Don't you like it? You're crying."

"I can't believe you did all of this . . . after you already got me the book."

"You do like it, don't you?"

I threw my arms around his thick neck. "It's everything I've ever dreamed of! How did you do this?!"

"I knew you'd love it!" Brontes laughed. His strong arms wrapped around my waist, lifting me up and spinning me around in a joyous swirl. "I built it for you, but that's our little secret."

"Thank you! Thank you, Brontes! Thank you!" I buried my face into his chest, blinking back tears. "Why would you do this for me?"

"Isn't it obvious by now?" Brontes smiled softly, his large hands rubbing my back, his dark blue eyes staring through my soul. "I love you, Gwyneira. I want to give you everything you could ever want and more."

I blinked at him. There was no use in fighting them any longer as the tears returned to my eyes at his words. Never had anyone valued me so deeply. My whole life, I had been a burden to my parents, to the Ice Kingdom, to the other servants, even to Fannar. But Brontes treasured me.

"You don't have to say it back," he said hastily. "You asked, so I'm just answering."

"I love you too." The words slipped out on their own, but as soon as they were spoken, I knew they were true. My heart, my life, my very soul belonged to this man.

With one swift movement, our lips pressed together, connecting in soft, adoring kisses. When we broke apart, I buried my face in his chest, listening to his heart hammer away. His smell washed over me, and I breathed it in.

Mmmm . . . it's so earthy . . . like sweet cedarwood. It made my mouth water. The heat of his breath fanned out down my neck, sending warmth through my body and between my legs.

"I love your hair, my sweet, beautiful snowflake." His fingers swept over the nape of my neck, causing goosebumps to rise all over my body. He slowly drew his hand out, lifting my long silver hair before letting it cascade back down, watching it in awe. "It looks like starlight."

Desire pooled within me, a flame ignited by his tender affection. My heart pounded wildly in my chest. Brontes' warm body was like a magnet. I longed to press myself against him, to feel every inch of him.

"So unbelievably beautiful. Ever since I laid eyes on you, I've been drawn to you like a moth to a flame."

My mind raced with thoughts of his lips on mine, the taste of his tongue, the feel of his strong, muscular body against my own, and the need to explore each and every contour of his skin with my fingertips. I bit down on my lower lip, unsure if I should give voice to the desire that threatened to consume me whole.

"Are you okay?" His lips brushed the top of my head.

I nodded, tilting my face up to meet his gaze. The intensity of his eyes stole my breath.

"Good." He cupped my cheek, tracing his thumb over my lower lip. "Because I'm not quite ready to let you go yet."

Heat flooded my veins at his words. I swallowed hard, my hands curling into his shirt. “I don’t want you to let me go.”

“Is that so?” His voice dropped, a husky rumble against my ear. He took my lobe between his teeth, nibbling gently.

A shockwave tore through me, and a squeak escaped my lips.

Brontes gave a low, throaty chuckle. “You’re killing me, Princess, the sounds you make . . .” His lips found my neck, kissing a scorching trail up to my jaw.

I squeaked again, my chest arching into him.

“The way you respond to my touch . . .”

The warmth of embarrassment flooded my face, yet the fire in my belly grew hotter with every passing second. His praise only stoked the flames higher. The very fabric of my being seemed to scream out for him, aching to be closer, to lose myself in the depths of his passion.

“I can’t get enough of you.” His voice was a low and husky whisper.

The back of his fingers caressed the side of my neck. The electric sensation traveled through me like wildfire, igniting every nerve ending with its searing heat. My body trembled with want, craving more of his touch.

And just like that, the dam broke. I crushed my mouth onto his, fierce and demanding with a raw hunger. Brontes responded instantly. His lips were all at once familiar and new, devouring me with a ferocity that left me dizzy and breathless. I parted my lips with a sigh, an invitation, and he accepted with a low groan.

His velvety tongue danced around mine. Its gentle caress left my insides awash with a warmth that blossomed and spread throughout my being. I dissolved in his arms as he explored the depths of my mouth, imbuing it with a delightful sweetness.

My hand slid into his deep black hair, so harsh in color and so irresistible. Little strands of hair tickled between my fingers like soft down in my palm.

I whimpered as he kissed my neck again and moved lower. My arms pulled him closer. I wanted him closer. I wanted him as close to me as I could have him.

He's so . . . hot!

I wanted his body heat to scald me. The heat echoed through me as his heaving chest pushed against my own.

Our bodies pressed against each other, and I reveled in the electric current that coursed through me at the contact. His proximity was intoxicating, awakening sensations within me that I had never experienced before.

Noises escaped me—loud moans, but I was wrapped up in too much pleasure to care.

My breath hitched as his fingers slid up my thigh, teasing the hem of my dress, his lips wandering farther down my chest. The anticipation was maddening, a delicious torment that left me craving more. Always more. Of him and the exquisite pleasure we found in each other's arms.

"Please," I shuddered, my body begging for his touch, my arousal reaching a fever pitch.

But suddenly, Brontes flinched in my arms and looked toward the door to his study.

My heart was beating so hard that I panted in his arms. "What's wrong?"

He listened carefully for a second. "Dammit. I think someone's coming into my study." Brontes looked at me apologetically before pecking me on the lips and then stepped back to leave. "I have to go. Enjoy the storage room." He gave me a wink before hurrying back to his study and closing the door behind him.

Though naturally disappointed that our fiery tryst had ended so abruptly, I looked around gratefully. There were worst places I could be than in the most stunning observatory I had ever seen.

And it was all mine.

CHAPTER THIRTEEN

I had never seen anything as amazing as the observatory I spent my days in between chores, absorbing *For the Love of Stars: A Study of the Cosmos*. By then, I must have read it cover to cover at least four times and gushed about its brilliance to Brontes endlessly, often bursting into his study next door to talk to him about something new I'd spotted in the text. I could tell he wasn't as deeply interested in the subject as I was, but he said my enthusiasm made him happy.

To be honest, though Fannar and I spent hours pretending to be playing with them, I was completely clueless as to how to use the orrery and telescopes that had been so enthralling in my textbooks. While it was daunting at first, I eagerly learned everything I could about the equipment. When I finally succeeded in tracking down the stars and constellations with my telescopes, I became absolutely giddy.

My observatory became my own world of refuge, where time seemed to stand still with its sheen of shining brass. But in reality, I kept losing track of time in between enjoying Brontes' company or studying the stars, including the night I had snuck in after dinner clean up. I didn't know how long I'd been there when I heard a double knock on the door to Brontes' study, followed by his head peeking in.

"Gwyneira, it's getting late," he said. "You need to get back to the servants' quarters, or they'll start worrying about you."

"Fine," I sighed as I pulled my face away from one of the telescopes.

He laughed and walked over to me, touching my elbow gently. "You can come back tomorrow!"

"I know, but I only get a few hours a night to see the stars—and it's so *beautiful* tonight!"

He looked up through the large glass window. I had already turned off the lights inside the observatory. The night was clear, and the stars were shining mightily from above, breaking the eternal darkness with their soft glow.

"It is," he agreed in awe.

"And you can see so many constellations! It is a picture-perfect sky!"

"Which ones can we see tonight?" He smiled at my joy.

"Come, sit with me!" I grabbed his large hand and pulled him toward the plush rug. "I'll show you!"

Brontes chuckled. "Fine, but then you need to go. We don't want anyone to find out about your secret storage room."

"It won't take long. I promise!"

We sat down on the rug together, facing the window, and I pointed out stars. "Do you see those three stars that form a triangle? Right there?"

"Oh, yes," Brontes said. "Is that Thasulla?"

"Yes! Xodall is her head, and Axeyar and Naneas are her shoulders."

"And," Brontes said slowly, as if accessing a distant memory, "Jhadea and Azphion below them form her body, right?"

"Yes! That's Qotlotl and Hadros, which form her legs."

Brontes frowned a little. "Where're her arms? I don't see them."

"She's holding them up." I held both my arms up to demonstrate. "Like this!"

As I did, Brontes took the opportunity to slide closer to me on the rug, head resting on my collarbone so my arms wound around him when I put them down.

"I see them now," he replied with a flirty smile.

"Brontes!" I giggled at his sly move. I tilted my head back, my eyes tracing the constellations that seemed to sprawl endlessly across the sky. "It's breathtaking."

"Much like you," he murmured, brushing a stray lock of hair from my face.

The heat rose to my cheeks again as my pulse quickened. "Brontes," I whispered, unsure of what to say yet unable to look away from his smoldering gaze.

He leaned down, his lips brushing against mine, and then slowly caressed my arm, sending tingles of pleasure through me.

"Tell me . . ." His fingers played with my hair, his voice low and sultry like the embers of a dying fire. "What do you dream about, Princess?"

I nestled closer to him, feeling his heartbeat intensify under my ear. "I dream about you," I admitted.

He chuckled softly, his breath tickling my skin. "Is that so?"

Heat rose in my cheeks, and I averted my gaze, feeling shy and awkward as I spoke honestly. "I dream about your touch, your kiss, the way you make me feel wanted and alive."

Brontes grasped my chin and turned my face toward him. "I dream about you too. Every night, I dream about holding you like this, feeling you against me . . . and making you mine."

The boldness of his words sent a jolt coursing through my body. His eyes darkened with desire as they locked onto mine. Electricity hummed in the air between us. My heart pounded with a wild rhythm that urged me to give into his magnetic pull.

My breasts pressed against his chest, my lips parting in invitation. Brontes responded eagerly in a deep, passionate kiss with a fierce hunger. Our tongues explored one another in a slow, sensual rhythm. Our bodies molded together, the heat between us growing with every passing moment.

Moaning softly into his mouth, I clung to him, drowning in sensation, lost to the firm contours of his chest pressing against me, the taste of his lips and tongue, the scent of leather and spice that clung to his skin. All I wanted was to be closer to him, to feel the warmth of his body against mine. Every inch of his hard form pressed up against me. I yearned to lose myself in the storm of his passion, swept away by the intensity of his love.

My hands clawed at the fabric of his shirt, desperate to feel the sculpted planes of his chest beneath my fingertips.

He growled low in his throat, hands sliding down to grip my waist as he deepened the kiss. Brontes' hands roamed over my clothing, leaving a trail of fire in their wake as they wandered lower to squeeze my bottom and pull me closer to him.

A squeak escaped my lips as the hard length of his arousal pressed against me, causing my own longing to pool between my legs. I instinctively rocked against him, whimpering softly beyond thought, driven only by primal need.

Brontes broke the kiss. "Gwyneira," he breathed, his voice rough as he lowered my back gently onto the rug, his eyes never leaving mine. "I want—"

"Yes," I interrupted, reaching up to pull him down on top of me as I panted. "Anything. Everything."

My hands eagerly slid under his shirt, fingers splaying across his firm abs.

Brontes smiled sinfully and shed his shirt, revealing the hard, sculpted muscles of his chest and arms. Every inch of his body seemed like it had been carved from marble. My mouth watered at the sight, and I reached out to touch him, unable to believe that a man with such an awe-inspiring physique existed.

But he was faster. Brontes lowered his head, his lips finding mine once more. The kiss was slow and deep and thorough, stealing my breath and my senses until I was lost in the sweet, burning heat of his embrace. I slid my fingers into his hair, wrapping the silky strands around them.

My hands explored over his expansive shoulders and down his back, fingertips brushing faint ridges.

I broke away from his kiss, turning to get a better look at his back. My heart squeezed as I traced the raised scars that marked his tan skin, remembering the moment Brontes endured his parents' punishment for me.

"You bear the scars of battle," I murmured softly. "The price you paid for me."

"Not all of them," he glanced back at me. "But I'd do it all again, Gwyneira. A hundred times over for you."

Leaning forward, I pressed a gentle kiss to each scar, lingering on the largest. He shivered under my touch, his muscles tense beneath my lips.

My soft kisses continued down his broad back, and Brontes closed his eyes, tilting his head back with a deep, guttural groan. His chest rose and fell rapidly. His strong arms pulled me in front of him, and our mouths met in a passionate embrace.

He unfastened the buttons of my dress and broke our kiss to ease it over my head before letting it drift to the floor. I mewed softly as his hands slowly made their way up my body, gliding over my curves and lingering on the swell of my breasts. A chill passed over my body as his rough fingers skimmed over my skin.

He reached around to unclasp my bra, my breasts spilling out. His eyes slowly devoured my body, lingering on the curve of my waist and the fullness of my bosom before finally settling on my eyes.

"You're more beautiful than I ever dreamed of," he said with dark longing and admiration.

"I'm not." I frowned, wanting to cover my exposed breasts from his fiery gaze, but his words filled me with a sweet warmth.

"You are."

My hands reached up and wandered across the hard planes of his chest and shoulders, trying to memorize every curve and hollow. I ached to be one with him, the hard contours of his body melding into my eager curves as I tried to absorb every ounce of his being.

Brontes shuddered under my explorations, his grip on my hips tightening. A low growl rumbled in his chest. He crushed me closer, kissing me with a relentless ferocity that made my knees weak.

His hands moved slowly across my body, exploring every curve. Goosebumps rose on my arms, and I gasped as his touch sent liquid fire coursing through my veins.

"I want you so badly." My voice was so breathy I could barely get out the words.

Brontes made a low, hungry sound, nipping at my exposed shoulder. "I want you, too, Princess. You're all I've thought about for months. I want to know every inch of your body." His gaze lowered to my chest.

I shuddered as his hand palmed my plump bosom.

"I want to trace every curve with my tongue. To find out what makes you moan." He lowered his head to take one of my nipples into his mouth, causing me to gasp.

His tongue explored both until it settled on one, circling and flicking the tip.

"Oh, Brontes," I moaned and arched into him, my fingers fisting in his hair.

He continued to tease and suckle me, sending waves of delight coursing through my body as my lower belly burned with need. His mouth moved to my other peak, sucking and tugging at the sensitive bud. He had me breathless and delirious.

His hands moved over my body, stroking and kneading my soft curves. He reached the waist of my panties, sliding them off and tossing them aside.

His rough, warm hands moved up my legs, caressing the smooth skin of my inner thighs. I gasped sharply as his thumb touched my moist slit for the first time. He stroked it gently before easing a finger inside me. I gasped again at the sudden, unfamiliar sensation. Brontes rubbed his thumb over the sensitive nub between my legs, coaxing a moan from my lips. His head bent toward me, bringing his lips close to mine. I could feel his breath, warm and sweet, as his eyes seemed to gaze into my soul.

"Is this okay?" he asked gently. "Tell me to stop, and I will."

I shook my head franticly. "More. I want more."

Brontes growled low. His lips moved to my ear, whispering, "You feel so good, Princess. So tight and wet. I want to feel you come on my fingers."

Another finger slipped into me, filling me up and pushing against the inner walls of my body. His fingers brushed and stroked my sensitive insides, sending sparks of pleasure with every movement.

I whimpered, rocking my hips against his hands. His thumb worked in tandem with his other hand, his fingers plunging in and out, sending me to the edge of reason. I was so close.

"That's it, Princess," he breathed, his lips trailing down my neck. "Come for me."

"Brontes!" I cried out his name as his words sent me over the edge. I clung to him as he continued to move his fingers inside me, drawing out my orgasm.

He eased his fingers out when I stopped shaking. I was floating, utterly content and boneless on the rug. Slowly, my heartbeat steadied, and my breathing evened out.

Brontes smirked down at me. "Are you back?"

I nodded, a smile curving my own lips. "I'm here."

"Good, because we're not done yet." Heat flashed in his gaze, his eyes wickedly half-lidded as he took in my body. "Look at you. So beautiful. So perfect, Princess."

I blushed. Suddenly conscious again of my complete nakedness before him, my cheeks hot with embarrassment.

Brontes drew back a little. "I want you so badly," he murmured, brushing a lock of hair from my face and tucking it behind my ear.

I nodded, aching for him. "I want you too. I want this."

My body desperately craved his body. I wanted to feel him inside of me, to know what it would be like to have him take me. I'd never done this before, but I knew instinctively that he was the one who'd finally make me feel whole.

Brontes kissed my lips, his tongue finding mine in a slow, passionate kiss.

"Are you sure? It's your first time," he asked gently, his breath warm against my wet skin. His question was full of concern and tenderness.

"More than anything," I replied, my voice steadier than I expected it to be.

"I promise I'll go slow. I'll make you feel good," he whispered, his voice husky and low. His eyes were filled with adoration. "I'm going to make it as perfect as possible."

"I know you will." I nodded, my heart beating rapidly in my chest.

Brontes stood, the muscles of his statuesque body tense and rigid as they glistened in the moonlight. "You have no idea how much I've wanted to make you mine," he growled as he undid his belt and pants, letting them fall to the floor, revealing his large, thick erection.

The coil of arousal in my belly wound tighter, and more heat bloomed between my legs. I wanted to touch it, to feel it pulsing between my fingers, but instead, I lay still, my heart racing in anticipation as he lowered himself onto me.

I swallowed the lump in my throat. I'd never been so turned on in my life, wanting him more than I ever thought possible, my entire being consumed by the need to feel him inside me, to have him claim me as his own.

His hands slid down to grip my thighs, spreading them wider as he settled between my legs. He positioned the hard length of his manhood at my entrance, pressing against my folds. My breath hitched at the contact, a jolt of ecstasy shooting through me. My inner muscles clenched in anticipation, and I tried to steady my breath.

"Yes, Brontes," I whispered, my voice full of need and desire. "Please . . ."

I gasped loudly as he filled me slowly inch by inch until he was fully seated inside me.

His fingers dug into my thighs as he held himself there, my body adjusting to his size. His enormous girth felt amazing. I'd always been told that it would hurt the first time, but I didn't feel pain, only pleasure. I was made for this. Made for Brontes. We fit together like two pieces of a puzzle. I was made to be his.

"Gwyneira, you feel so good," Brontes said with a rough voice, pushing further against me, causing me to squeal.

Brontes took advantage of my parted lips with a wild and fierce kiss. His tongue ravaged my mouth hungrily, our tongues tangling in a passionate dance.

As he moved his hips slowly against mine, I moaned into his mouth as euphoria began to build up inside me.

"Brontes," I murmured, my fingernails digging into his back, bracing myself for more as he took me.

With each thrust, he stretched me wider and deeper with his hard length. I moaned, my body moving in sync with his on its own.

He leaned back and cupped my breasts. I mewed and arched my back, savoring the unbelievable feeling of his length inside of me. His fingertips scorched my skin as they ran over my nipples. I'd never felt anything so wonderful.

From where I lay beneath him, Brontes' body was a breathtaking wall of muscle, taut and rock-hard. His broad chest heaved as he quickened the pace, his hips vigorously pumping against me, and his biceps bulged with each thrust.

The weight of his lustful eyes stared at me intensely as he drove into me harder, watching devilishly as he ravished my body.

"You are mine now, Gwyneira," he grunted. "You belong to me."

The possessive claim sent a thrill through me. I was his, now and always, bound to him body and soul.

"Yours," I echoed breathlessly. "Only yours."

My words awoke the beast that lay dormant inside him. He grabbed my hips tightly, yanking me closer as he plunged into me with a ferocity I could scarcely bear. I moaned, my hands gripping the fibers of the rug beneath me.

He pounded relentlessly against me, pushing my body to its limit with every chaotic stroke until I was shaking uncontrollably.

"Yes," I panted as I became lost in the strength of his powerful hips slamming into my body, my breasts bouncing in sync.

His skin glistened with sweat as he moved, faster and faster, his thrusts becoming more frantic and desperate. My body tensed, my muscles contracted. My breath came in short, sharp gasps. I clung desperately to him, moaning and trembling with the need for him to take me completely.

The intensity of his lust reverberated through him as he pushed me further and further. Never had I felt so desired. He was so close now, throbbing inside me, crushing against the deepest part of me in a delirious stretch.

He looked down at me with ravenous eyes and asked in a gravelly, husky voice, "Do you want me to come inside of you?"

"Yes," I gasped. "Please, I want it. All of it."

His lips curved into a seductive half-smile at my response. He propelled his hard length into me one last time, and I gasped, my fingernails digging into his forearms.

"Gwyneira," he groaned, his entire body stiffened as he closed his eyes.

I cried out as his member pulsated, and he spilled his seed into me.

It was unlike anything I had ever felt before. The hot and intense sensation spread through every inch of my body like wildfire, setting free an immense wave of bliss that crashed over me.

He leaned over. His chiseled form shuddered against me as his heart hammered in his chest, his masculinity still locked inside me. I was full of him, and my body was finally complete.

"Gwyneira," he whispered, showering my face with soft kisses.

"Mmmm," I purred in contentment, my entire being still tingling.

Brontes collapsed next to me and wrapped me in his arms. After a moment, he pressed a tender kiss to my brow and smiled down at me.

"I love you, my snowflake," he said with so much affection that it made my heart ache.

From that moment, I knew he would be the only man I'd ever want. We belonged to each other, two halves of a whole, and nothing could ever tear us apart.

"I love you too, my Brontes," I whispered, tracing the strong line of his jaw.

Brontes pulled me against him, and I leaned into his embrace, resting my head on his chest to listen to the steady beat of his heart.

Time stood still as our love blossomed like a rose unfurling beneath the light of the moon. There was no beginning and no end, no before and no after, only this single eternal moment that bound us together forever.

The last of my doubts and fears melted away, burned to ashes in the flames of his devotion. We were no longer two souls adrift, struggling through the darkness. We were one, and it was more than anything I had ever dreamed of in my lonely tower room. An epic romance, a handsome prince, and a love as vast and infinite as the cosmos itself.

My fairytale had come to life at last.

CHAPTER FOURTEEN

I scrubbed vigorously at the stubborn sauce stain on the counter, my hands aching from the effort. Beside me, Maisol washed the mountain of dishes we'd accumulated during the lunch service, her sleeves rolled up to avoid the soapy water. Rori mopped the floor, carefully maneuvering around the other kitchen staff, including Dagur, who took inventory of the ingredients needed for dinner. The air in the kitchen was thick with the scent of cleaning supplies mixed with the lingering aromas of the previous meal we'd prepared.

"Rori, make sure you get that spot near the stove," I said, pointing with my free hand. She nodded and steered the mop in the direction I indicated, a concentrated look on her face.

"Gwyn, you've done a great job washing the pans this time," Maisol commented, glancing over her shoulder at me. "You're definitely getting the hang of this whole 'kitchen duty' thing."

"Thanks, Maisol." A small smile tugged at my lips as I realized that I was strangely content.

As a princess betrothed to the heir of the Storm Kingdom, working as a scullery maid certainly wasn't where I envisioned myself to be—yet I couldn't help but be grateful for my new friends and finally being able to pull my own weight.

"Alright, ladies," Dagur announced as he checked a final item off his list. "I think we're almost done here."

We all took a step back, admiring our handiwork. The kitchen gleamed, every surface now spotless and inviting.

"Princess Gwyneira," a soft voice called from the doorway, causing us all to turn. A handmaid stood there, her eyes downcast as she curtsied. "The prince has requested your presence for dinner with the royal family."

My heart quickened at the unexpected invitation—I hadn't dined with Brontes and his parents since that horrible day when he'd been lashed in my stead. The memory of the whip cracking against his flesh still haunted me. Why would the king and queen want me to come to dinner again? A mixture of excitement and nerves bubbled within me.

"Go on, Gwyneira," Rori urged, smiling encouragingly. "We can handle the rest."

"Are you sure?" I asked, feeling guilty for leaving them behind.

Maisol nodded as well, sharing a knowing look with the others. "Of course," she said. "You deserve this. Enjoy dinner with Prince Brontes."

"Thank you."

With a grateful smile, I followed the handmaid out of the kitchen and down the hallway. She led me to a chamber where several other handmaids awaited, each one ready to help transform me from a kitchen maid back into the princess I truly was.

As soon as I entered, the handmaids scurried about as they prepared a bath and laid out an array of dresses for me to choose from. The warm perfumed water enveloped my body as I slipped into the tub, steam curling around me like tendrils of smoke. It was a luxury I hadn't experienced in far too long. The simple act of bathing was now imbued with a sense of decadence.

"Your hair has grown so much," one handmaid noted as she began running a brush through my wet tresses after my bath. "Shall we style it up or leave it down?"

"Up, please," I replied, imagining how elegant my neck would look when exposed. My thoughts drifted to Brontes, wondering if he'd find the sight alluring.

"Of course, Your Highness." Her fingers danced deftly through my hair, twisting and pinning until a delicate chignon took shape at the nape of my neck, and adorned it with a myriad of tiny crystals.

Another handmaid approached, carrying a tray with various pots of makeup. She applied a light dusting of powder to my face, followed by a subtle sweep of blush across my cheeks, giving me a rosy glow that made me feel radiant.

"Your eyes need something special," she mused, delicately applying a shimmering shade of ice blue to my eyelids. I blinked, feeling the light weight of the makeup on my skin.

"Thank you," I murmured, admiring her handiwork in the mirror before me. The transformation was remarkable—I looked like royalty once more.

"Finally, let's find you a dress." A third handmaid gestured toward the selection laid out for me. I hesitated, unsure which would best capture Brontes' attention.

"May I suggest this one?" She held up a gown of deep sapphire silk, the color reminiscent of the night sky. "It would accentuate your eyes beautifully."

"Perfect," I agreed, remembering the deep connection Brontes and I shared with the stars as she helped me slip into the dress. The fabric clung to my curves, hugging my waist and hips before flaring out in a gentle cascade of silk.

"Stunning," one handmaid breathed as they all stepped back to admire their handiwork.

"Thank you, ladies," I said appreciatively. "I think he's going to love it."

About fifteen minutes later, my heart raced in my chest as I paced nervously back and forth in the chamber, fiddling with my dress absentmindedly as I waited for Brontes to arrive. Would the Storm King and Queen accept me this time? What if they didn't approve of my appearance? My mind attempted to blaze through every etiquette lesson the queen had taught me. I looked down at my hands. *I need to stay in control of my powers. Not even a pinch of frost.*

The door creaked open, and Brontes stepped into the room. His mere presence washed a sense of calm over my anxious thoughts like a soothing balm. He smiled warmly at me, his eyes sweeping over my appearance.

"You look absolutely stunning, Gwyneira," he said, his voice sincere and tender.

I gave a shy smile—unsure if I'd ever get used to Brontes' loving compliments. Looking down at my dress bashfully, it felt luxurious against my skin, which had grown accustomed to the harsh fabric of the servants' uniform.

Brontes closed the distance between us and pressed a long, tender kiss to my lips, leaving behind an electrifying sensation that lingered on them.

"So," Brontes began as he pulled away from our kiss. "My parents don't know you're joining us for dinner tonight."

"What? Are you serious?" I straightened my back in alarm, and my stomach churned with apprehension. "Is this a good idea?"

"It'll be okay." He squeezed my hand and gave me a determined stare. "You're a princess, my fiancée, and future queen of this kingdom. I won't let them disrespect you this time."

I hesitated, biting my lower lip.

"Don't worry. I'll handle their reactions. Just stay by my side and follow my lead."

"Okay," I agreed. Though still concerned, I admired his resolve for me to be treated as more than just a servant.

"Are you ready?" He extended a bent arm toward me.

With a deep breath, I nodded. "Let's do this." I grasped his firm bicep, and he escorted me from the chamber.

Brontes led me through the winding corridors of the castle, our footsteps echoing softly off the cold stone walls.

As we approached the grand doors of the dining room, anxiety crept into my veins once more.

"Your Majesties, His Royal Highness Prince Brontes and Her Royal Highness Princess Gwyneira," the head butler announced as we entered the room.

The Storm King and Storm Queen sat at the table, their expressions somber, faces set like masks. Upon hearing my name, their heads swiveled immediately to face us. The Storm Queen's expression morphed into a blend of shock and anger, her eyes narrowing dangerously as she glared at me, and I bristled under her gaze.

"Brontes," she growled. "What is the meaning of this? Why is that hideous Ice Enchanted here?"

"She's eating with us tonight," he replied calmly.

I nibbled my lower lip apprehensively.

"Why?" The king asked stonily. "She caused a scene last time."

"*I* caused a scene—don't blame her," Brontes said.

"She was disrespectful." The queen added.

"And I was more so!" Brontes insisted. "Yet I still eat with you."

"You're royalty," the king said.

"So is she!" Brontes snapped.

"Brontes," the Storm Queen hissed, her face contorted with rage. "I did not give you permission to bring her to dinner."

"Mother, I am taking my betrothal to Gwyneira seriously," Brontes declared, his voice becoming steady again. "She is a princess and my future wife. As my fiancée, she belongs at my side eating with us, not in a barn with servants."

The Storm Queen's chest rose and fell rapidly, simmering with anger beneath her regal exterior. I braced myself for her wrath.

"You dare defy your queen, ungrateful child?!" She spat the words out like venom.

Her fist pounded onto the table with a loud slam, causing the dishes and silverware to shake and rattle, making me flinch. But Brontes' grip on my arm tightened, reassuring me as he met his mother's glare head-on.

"This is about respecting our alliance with the Ice Kingdom." He locked eyes with his mother, his voice firm and unyielding in his reasoning. "They have given us their princess. It is our responsibility to treat her with the respect and dignity she deserves. If word got out to the Ice Kingdom about how you've been treating her, they may sever our alliance or, worse, threaten war."

Though I questioned if my parents would really care about how I was being treated, I didn't speak a word. The tension in the air crackled like lightning as the Storm King's eyes flicked back and forth between his wife and son, listening to their heated debate.

As the Storm Queen opened her mouth to argue again, the Storm King finally spoke up.

"Good to see you taking this situation seriously for once, son." The king's deep voice echoed through the dining hall. "I commend your dedication to our alliance and your commitment to your duties as a prince. Very well. She may eat with us."

The queen's eyes widened with disbelief and indignation, her jaw clenching tightly. "But, my king—"

"Enough, my queen," the Storm King interrupted, his voice rumbling like thunder. "I have made my decision. Gwyneira will stay for dinner."

Brontes nodded, relaxing a little. "Thank you, Father."

With a final nod from the Storm King, the queen acquiesced, but her anger silently boiled beneath the surface. Her lips pressed into a thin line, and she glared at us as we took our seats at the royal table, her eyes icy daggers that promised retribution.

"Let us eat," the Storm King declared before raising his goblet to his lips.

As the meal commenced, the sound of silverware clinking against fine porcelain permeated the still air.

I stole a glance at Brontes, sitting beside me. My heart surged with pride and appreciation that he'd stood up for our relationship against his own mother. Though the queen clearly seethed quietly, I whispered a silent prayer of gratitude to the gods.

Maybe this will be the start of a better relationship with his parents.

CHAPTER FIFTEEN

I pushed the end of the shovel into the pile of horse manure, trying to scoop it up onto the shovel.

Elias laughed at me. "No, you need to use your arms!"

"But my hands hurt!" I whined.

I looked at my palms. Just below the lowest joints of my fingers were red and raw blisters. Splinters studded my hands where I'd held the decrepit tool.

Elias looked and sucked in a breath through his teeth.

"Oh . . . Yes, that's the start of stable hands."

He offered his own. There were hard callouses all over his hands. "See?" Elias laughed again and scooped the waste I'd been struggling with.

"I'm not surprised!" He chuckled. "The question is why a princess is down here scooping horse crap in the first place."

Unfortunately, I knew the answer. The dinner went exceptionally well. The king, whose face had always been so solemn and stern before, had started to smile more often and even asked me a few questions. As for the Storm Queen, her displeasure made it clear that she hadn't appreciated the king's cordial behavior toward me. In the days that followed, my workload increased, and the worst tasks were suddenly assigned to me.

In additional to cooking and cleaning, she had me cleaning toilets—the castle had a lot of toilets. A few days ago, she caught me laughing in the kitchen with Maisol and Rori, so she assigned even more physical labor, including mucking the stables.

On the bright side, I didn't get a chance to see Elias all that often . . . and he was doing most of the work for me.

"So, are you here forever, or are you going to be reassigned again?" Elias asked, scooping up horse dung and piling it into the wheelbarrow.

"I'm not sure." I shrugged. "The queen keeps moving me around. If she thinks this task isn't humiliating enough, she'll switch me again."

Elias nodded. "The queen does not like losing control of the household, and you have certainly upset the balance in the castle."

"Unfortunately for her, I have friends all over the castle now, so I can find something to enjoy in any chore she assigns me."

He laughed loudly. "She's trying so hard to make you miserable, but no matter where she puts you, you find some way to be happy."

I grinned at the thought. "That's right! She can't break my spirit!" I declared with determination.

We both laughed for a moment.

"The queen has never done a chore in her life," Elias snickered. "So I guess she thinks that making a princess work with us *lower lifeforms* would be the worst thing she could possibly do. I won't lie. It's very satisfying to watch her be so wrong."

I sank down a little bit. "No, the worst thing is that she's been watching me so closely that Brontes and I haven't had a chance to be alone together. The only time I see him is during dinner, but it's impossible for us to be ourselves with the king and queen present."

He gave me a sympathetic look and picked up the wheelbarrow. He began wheeling it away, and I carried both our shovels to follow him.

"That's true. I'm sorry about that. I don't understand why she would arrange your betrothal just to keep you two separated."

"Me either."

Elias tipped the wheelbarrow up, and I shoveled its contents into the compost pile.

"There must be something we can do to help." Elias mused out loud. "I mean, we know everything about this castle and what happens here. That's what the royals don't seem to realize." He smirked. "They never pay attention to us and treat us like we're just part of the furniture, but in reality, we notice everything. So if there is anything we can do to help, let us know."

"Really? You think the others would help me, even though I'm a royal too?"

"Of course, Gwyneira," Elias said, putting the wheelbarrow back down and turning around. "You're always willing to help and never acted like you're better than a *lowly* servant. You're one of us now, and we take care of our own. Plus, it'll drive the queen crazy if you're happy!" He laughed. "If you need something, all you need to do is ask, and someone will help."

Hearing him say that they considered me one of their own made me smile, especially since I had long considered them all as my friends, having embraced me and welcomed me into their world with open arms.

"Thank you, Elias. That means a lot." There wasn't anything I could think of at the moment, but I appreciated the offer immensely. "If I think of something, I'll let you know."

The queen did her best to keep me occupied from sunrise to bedtime. Even when I was able to sneak away to the observatory, I rarely saw Brontes there. He either wasn't in his study or was there with other people, so I'd have to keep myself quietly hidden.

Dinner continued to be the only time I consistently saw Brontes. Despite being under the disapproving gaze of the Storm Queen, I savored stealing glances with Brontes and treasured the warmth of his hand on mine under the table.

This went on for weeks. I missed being alone with Brontes so much. Eventually, my excitement about the observatory dwindled to such an extent that I actually spent time dusting it. Without him, it became an empty chamber haunted by the ghosts of our passionate rendezvous, overlooking a dark sky where the stars used to sparkle when we were together.

I longed for the comforting warmth of Brontes' presence, the feeling of his skin against mine as we embraced, giving me a sense of security and safety. A longing that seemed to grow each day made me restless, like I had to be near him to feel complete.

As I polished the furniture in the hallway near the observatory, a loud *CRASH* outside startled me, making me jump. Once I had regained my composure, I rushed to the window to locate the source of the sound. When I peered out, I was surprised to see Brontes practicing his powers in the courtyard.

"Brontes!" I shouted down to him, waving my arms frantically. "Brontes!" I called out louder, but he didn't respond.

Disappointed, I realized I must be too far away for him to hear or see me. I watched for a few more minutes, admiring his growing mastery of his abilities.

An idea suddenly came to me. I gestured with my hands toward one of the clouds that Brontes created until snowflakes slowly began to drift down from it.

When he noticed the falling snow, Brontes held out his palm and looked up at the cloud. He looked around excitedly, trying to locate me. I waved from the window again, and his head turned up in my direction. When he finally saw me, a wide grin spread across his face, and he eagerly walked toward the window.

"Gwyneira!" He called up to me, looking delighted at seeing me again. "I knew my snowflake must be around somewhere."

"I'm glad I finally got your attention, Brontes!" I smiled back down at him. "Aren't you worried the queen will see you using your powers in court?"

He shrugged. "My parents are gone for a few hours on royal business. If someone tattles on me, then I can figure out who their spies are."

I just wish I could see him up close . . .

As I let the thought pass through my mind, my powers pulsed within me, reminding me what I was capable of.

I had never attempted this particular feat before. Such a large display of magic outside of the servants' quarters would surely have drawn attention, so I couldn't risk it. However, I had watched my brother do it many times in the Ice Kingdom. Taking a deep breath, I closed my eyes and recalled how he used to do it.

"Hey, Gwyneira!" My brother called from the ground outside of my tower, then put his palms together. As I watched, a small frost crept over his palms. As he separated them, he took his finger and wrote my name in the frost of his hand. I was thrilled.

Fannar clenched his hands in front of him and closed his eyes in concentration. The air around him began to shimmer, and an icy mist swirled around his arms and legs. He opened his eyes and gestured one hand as if drawing a spiral in the air. An ice ramp emerged from the ground, weaving and twisting until it reached the window of my tower. Fannar easily hurried up the ramp and climbed into my room.

"Wow, Fannar!" I exclaimed. "That's amazing!"

"Wait until I start attending the academy!" He replied excitedly. "I'll be able to do so much more!"

"I can't wait until I'm old enough to go to the academy too. I'll study the stars and learn to use my powers once I get them!"

Fannar laughed fondly and tousled my hair when I did. "I bet you'll become a top scholar of the cosmos!"

"Oh, that would be wonderful!" I cheered. "I know we'll be in different years, but can we study together?"

"Sure, but fair warning. I'm not letting my younger sis outrank me!" Fannar joked.

A wave of wistfulness washed over me as I remembered my older brother, along with the aching feeling of knowing that I hadn't seen him in ages. The fact that we were apart only amplified my admiration for him.

I focused on the memory of Fannar summoning the ice bridge. *How did he do it?*

My gaze fixed intently on my palms until they became illuminated in an arctic, bluish-white glow. A frigid mist swirled around my outstretched arms, and I placed my hands on the window ledge. Then, in a burst of light, an awe-inspiring ice bridge curled and corkscrewed its way from the window to the ground in front of Brontes.

He stepped onto it, cautiously at first to test the stability, and began walking up the frozen surface, confident in his footing at first, but soon he lost his grip as the incline grew steeper. He chuckled lightly as he attempted to dig his fingers into the ice to try to slow his descent. Eventually, he slid downward slowly like a cat against curtains.

I giggled. Walking over ice was easy for an Ice Enchanted, but it had never occurred to me that other Enchanted wouldn't fair as well. I formed stairs beside the ramp to make it easier for Brontes to scurry up.

Soon, his wonderful face appeared in the window, and he climbed through it into the hallway. He immediately pulled me into a tight embrace, the strength of his arms wrapping around me as we melted into each other. I buried my face in the crook of his neck, breathing in the comforting scent of him.

After a few moments, he pulled away and gazed at me with his beautiful navy-blue eyes. "Are you okay?" he asked urgently. "She hasn't hurt you, has she?"

I shook my head. "No. She's just had me in the stables for a while." I opened my palms to him, showing him all the callouses that had built up over the weeks of hard labor. "Elias says I have stable hands now."

I said it proudly, but his face was etched with sadness and despair. "My Gwyneira . . ." He took my hands and kissed my palms, running his fingers over the callouses for a few moments and growing more melancholic every second he stared at them. "Forcing the future queen to work in the stables." He shook his head. "You shouldn't have to. You deserve a life without hardship, my sweet snowflake."

"It's not too bad." I shrugged. "I just miss you terribly."

Brontes leaned forward. Our lips pressed together, and the tip of his tongue touched mine. When he broke, he looked deeply into me.

"Can you hold on a little longer?" he asked. "I'm still working with Father to try to calm Mother down. He's the only one who can get her to back down at this point."

I nodded.

Brontes looked up at the sky, still filled with dark clouds dropping light snow. "If Father can't get Mother to change her ways, then . . . well, I can't keep letting this happen to you." His brows furrowed as he answered himself firmly. "I told you I was going to make your life better, and here you are . . ." He touched my hands, shaking his head at the callouses on them. "Getting *stable hands.*"

"It's okay."

"It's not okay. I promised myself I'd make your life better." He kissed my palms gently again.

"Why are you so determined to make my life better?" I tilted my head in curiosity.

Brontes' dark eyes pierced through me as he paused before answering with a soft but steadfast voice.

"Because you understand," he began. "Everyone treats me like a monster. My parents think that my powers are too dangerous, and the servants avoid me. I don't blame them since I almost . . ." Brontes sighed heavily.

"That wasn't your fault," I said firmly, gripping his hands tightly.

"I know that now, but it's been this way for so many years that I started to believe it myself." He looked deeply into my eyes and cupped my face in his hands. "But then you came along. You're the only one who truly sees me. You see the man behind the monster."

"There is no monster, Brontes."

He smiled at me softly. "You are everything to me. I know we were brought together by our crazy families, but I can't imagine my life without you now. I love you, my princess."

His words warmed my heart as I leaned closer to him. "I love you too, my prince," I whispered.

"You deserve so much more than this. I promised you before that I'd give you a good life, and I swear to you, I'll keep that promise. No matter what it takes."

His head lowered, and his forehead rested on mine. We stayed like that for a few moments, lost in each other's eyes.

Gently, I reached out and ran my fingers lightly over the back of his neck, feeling each muscle ripple under my touch. His eyes closed, savoring the sensation, and he leaned into me ever so slightly, causing my heart to race in response.

As he raised his head, his stormy eyes locked onto mine with an intensity that ignited a fire within me.

"I'll make it up to you," he said with a smirk. "I'll make it up to you in ways you could never imagine."

As his hand trailed up my arm, electric tingles buzzed through my entire being, sending my nerve endings into overdrive. My body responded to his touch on its own, and I knew that I was powerless to resist him.

Brontes leaned in closer, his lips brushing against mine in a tantalizingly light touch. A soft moan escaped through my parted lips as I wrapped my arms around his neck, pulling him closer to me.

As our lips met in a fiery kiss, his hand moved to the small of my back, pulling me tightly against him. My desire for him grew with each passing second, a wild tempest threatening to break free from its confines. The emotions swirling within me were overwhelming yet exhilarating—a heady mix that left me breathless and wanting more. I couldn't contain myself any longer. I wanted nothing more than to lose myself in him and never let go.

"Did you say your parents are gone for a few hours?" I asked coyly.

"Yeah," he murmured.

"Come on then," I giggled, pulling him toward the observatory. "We don't have much time."

CHAPTER SIXTEEN

"Come here," Brontes said in a low rumble that instantly tightened the coil deep in my belly.

I eagerly closed the distance between us, pressing my lips against his.

As our mouths danced together, I reached for the hem of his shirt, hungry to explore his body. He lifted his arms, allowing me to pull it off. I ran my hands over the well-defined muscles that flexed and shifted beneath my palms, trailing from his biceps to his broad shoulders, then down to his chiseled chest and abs. It had been weeks since we'd last touched each other like this. I couldn't get enough.

"Your hands are so cold," he flinched slightly, but his eyes held a playful glint. "But I like it. I love feeling your hands on me."

"Brontes . . ." The sound of his name on my lips fueled my desire further, and for a moment, I pulled back from our heated kiss to study him.

My hands trailed up his arm and over his wide shoulders. My fingers slowly traced the curve of his collarbone, and as they did, a dark, black thundercloud with a light blue snowflake in its center appeared just beneath the right collarbone—his Enchanted mark.

"Wait, why do you have two Enchanted marks?" I asked, curiosity bubbling up amidst my lustful haze.

He glanced down at it, realizing that it appeared, and shrugged. "I don't know. I tried looking it up in the castle library, but all I could find was that they call it a 'Combined Enchanted mark.' Not much else."

"Interesting . . ." I whispered, still enthralled by the sight of it, when I realized, "Come to think of it. I've never even looked at my own mark before."

A wicked grin spread across Brontes' face. "Well then, let's change that, shall we?"

With surprising speed, he stripped me of my clothing, leaving me standing naked before him.

"You didn't have to take off all my clothes to see my mark!" I exclaimed with a laugh.

"I know." He smirked, his hot gaze roaming over my body. "But it's more fun."

He picked up a handheld mirror from one of the bookshelves and passed it to me. I gazed into its reflection, positioning it to where my mark would appear. Brontes stood behind me.

I purred as his strong hands slowly caressed my body, itching their way up from the side of my hips, over my arms, until finally reaching my collarbone. He pressed his hand to my chest, and the warmth from his hand spread across my skin.

"Look," he breathed, and I glanced into the mirror again to see my own mark appear—a light blue snowflake with a thundercloud inside of it, the opposite of Brontes'. "You have a Combined Enchanted mark too."

"Wow," I murmured.

"I'm glad to see one on you too."

"Why?"

He gave a dry laugh. "My parents always told me that having two marks is unnatural. It was proof that I'm a monster, too dangerous to use my powers."

I looked over my shoulder at him sadly, but he softly smiled back at me, brushing his fingers over my mark.

"Obviously, if you have one too, there's no way it means that I'm a monster," he continued, gently combing his fingers through my long white hair. "You're the gentlest person I've ever met."

The smile returned to my lips. "It just means that we're even more connected than we thought."

"Yes," Brontes whispered as he lowered his head to plant a trail of kisses along my neck and collarbone. His hands began exploring my body once more, leaving trails of fire in their wake. His fingers explored my mark again, and he paused for a moment before speaking softly in my ear, "You know this just means you're even more special to me, right?"

I nodded silently, too overwhelmed to speak.

Brontes' warm hands roamed my body, and a little moan escaped my lips as he touched me. Abruptly, I felt a pinch on my back. My heart leapt in surprise, and a rush of excitement flooded through me as I instinctively yelped, causing Brontes to jerk away from me.

"Oh, no!" he said quickly. "I'm so sorry!"

"What was that?" I asked.

"My powers . . . I think. Since I was just using them, it's still running through me. I didn't mean to shock you." He started to pull away. "Maybe we shouldn't—"

"Wait!" I protested, grasping his arm. "I-I don't mind it."

"No, I don't want to hurt you."

"But," I said shyly, "what if like it?"

He stared blankly at me for a moment before breaking into a smile. "Really?" he smirked.

Brontes slowly trailed two fingers down my arm, and I could see the sparks of electricity before they grazed my skin. I winced with anticipation, pain, and pleasure—it was hard to tell the difference. My eyes fluttered as a jolt of adrenaline rushed through me, and I gasped in delight.

A wicked grin spread across his face, and he chuckled a little. "Well, if you like it, then . . ."

Desire flared in his eyes as he leaned in, capturing my lips once more, while his hands returned to their exploration. His fingers slowly brushed my skin in a feather-light caress, and I flinched in anticipation. Brontes chuckled devilishly as each small shock elicited a squeak from me.

Brontes' eyes lingered on my bust as it heaved from my quickening breath and racing heart. He watched transfixed as I panted, lustfully taking in every curve.

My breath hitched as his large hands encircled both of my breasts. His calloused thumbs moved in circular motions, kneading and stroking them with unrestrained hunger. I gasped, my nipples hardening under his ruthless touch.

As I mewed and arched my back, his hands tightened, clamping down on my breasts even harder. His rough fingertips slid across my pebbled peaks. He squeezed them, rolled them, pulled them, rippling waves of bliss through my body. He was no longer just caressing me but claiming me as his own.

A spark shocked one of my nipples.

"Oh!" I gasped, and for a moment, I couldn't breathe as the sensation shot through my chest directly into the place between my legs. When I caught my breath again, it escaped from my mouth as a long moan.

A low, deep growl came from the back of Brontes' throat.

"Turn around," he ordered firmly, and I complied.

His breath tickled my skin as he lowered his head, each exhale a warm brush against my chest. His mouth closed around my nipple, insistent suction creating a delicious, unyielding pull that made me moan. His tongue bathed the sensitive bud with little circles as it gently shocked me again, the electric buzz causing me to cry out and writhe beneath him.

The ache between my legs grew unbearable. I pushed Brontes away from me.

"You're still wearing too much clothes," I panted with a coy smile, tracing the bulge straining inside his pants.

A low growl rumbled in his chest as he captured my lips again, devouring my mouth with a ferocious hunger. My core clenched in response, heat pooling once more between my legs.

My hands moved hastily to unfasten his pants and pulled them down, freeing his throbbing erection.

I dropped to my knees and wrapped my fingers around his length. He grunted as my tongue swirled around the tip, teasing him until I took him in my mouth. A guttural groan escaped him, and the delicious taste of his manhood filled my mouth.

"Look at me," he commanded forcefully, his voice rough with desire.

I opened my eyes and looked up at him as I stroked and sucked him.

"Gods, Gwyneira . . ." he rasped, his fingers tangling in my hair as he watched me bob up and down his masculinity. His hips twitched involuntarily, and his shaft pulsated against my tongue.

He tasted rich and intoxicating, driving me to take him deeper. I wanted to give him all the pleasure I could. For a moment, I thought he was about to spill his seed in my mouth.

"Fuck," he groaned, but he pulled me off before he could climax. "Stop, Gwyneira, or this will be over too soon."

Brontes pulled me up into his powerful chest and lifted me off the floor. I wrapped my legs around his waist so his manhood pressed against me. He effortlessly carried me over to the map table, the muscles in his arms rippling with strength, and set me down on the edge. His hands guided me onto my back, and he leaned over me.

"How can anyone be so beautiful?" he murmured.

My arms instinctively flew over my body in shame, feeling exposed and vulnerable.

Brontes pulled my arms apart and pinned them over my head. His fierce, lust-darkened eyes claimed my nakedness, setting fire to my very center, and made my body soak for him.

"Brontes," I whined under his labored breath, my legs trembling from the building heat within me.

"Tell me what you want, Princess," he whispered, pressing his forehead against mine, his dark eyes filled with craving.

"Make me yours," I pleaded, my voice barely more than a breathy whisper.

His lips curled into a predatory smile. "Like this?" He slipped a hand between my thighs, the heat of his skin searing my bare flesh.

"Please," I begged, my hips bucking.

"Patience, Princess," he chastised softly with a wicked gleam in his eyes. His fingertips danced over my slick folds, teasing me mercilessly. "Gods, Gwyneira. You're so wet for me." The sound of his husky voice only served to heighten my arousal.

Two of his fingers dipped inside me, making me cry out in ecstasy as he pumped them in and out while his thumb expertly stroked my most sensitive skin. His mouth latched onto my bosom again, searing my skin as his tongue frantically lashed against one nipple and the other. He pulled them deep into his mouth, eagerly sucking each one as if he could not get enough.

"Gods, yes!" I cried out. My vision blurred as the coil within me tightened, every nerve in my body on fire.

My hands gripped the edge of the table, writhing under the onslaught of sensation. His tongue worked its magic on my breasts, and his fingers continued its relentless assault on my womanhood, skillfully driving me close to the brink of ecstasy.

"Please . . . I need you inside me," I begged, desperate for him to fill me completely.

Without another word, he flipped me onto my stomach and yanked my hips down to meet his. My breasts pressed against the cold table as he took me from behind, driving himself into me in one jolting thrust and causing me to gasp with euphoric surprise. We moaned in unison at the feeling of being joined again.

"Gods, you feel amazing, Gwyneira," he growled.

His grip on my hips tightened possessively, and he drove himself into me over and over again with wild abandon, ravaging my body with a raw, unrelenting passion. The table rocked violently under us, but I didn't care. I relished the feeling of him pounding into me, stretching and filling me so completely. His deep, powerful thrusts stole any breath I had left until I was lost in a swirling sea of pleasure.

"Brontes . . . I'm so close," I moaned, feeling my climax rush toward me like a freight train.

He responded by increasing his pace. Bending me over on the map table even more, he slid a hand between my thighs, rubbing tight circles on the sensitive nub.

"Come for me, Princess," Brontes growled, and that was all it took.

"Brontes!" I cried out his name, clinging to him as I surrendered to the crashes of ecstasy sweeping through every cell of my being like an inferno.

My inner walls clenched around his member, tipping him into his completion.

"Fuck," Brontes grunted through gritted teeth, releasing his essence deep inside me before collapsing next to me.

We lay there together, breathlessly tangled in each other's arms on the map table for a long moment, waiting for the tremors to fade. Once his breathing slowed, Brontes scooped me off the map table, and I melted into his embrace, sated and euphoric in his arms. He placed me delicately on the floor rug and lay down beside me.

"I love you," he said softly, brushing a damp lock of hair from my forehead. "Things will get better. I have to believe that."

"I believe in us," I replied, cupping his face with my hand.

He nodded. "We'll face whatever comes our way. Together."

"Promise?" I asked, meeting his eyes.

"Promise," he answered, his dark eyes filled with resolve.

Brontes pulled me into his embrace. I nestled against him, savoring the warmth and solid strength of his body wrapped around mine. A dreamy lassitude stole over me as I slowly drifted off into a peaceful slumber in the contentment of his arms.

I woke up when Brontes ripped himself from our embrace. Lying on the rug, dozily blinking, I watched Brontes pull his shirt on and hastily fasten his pants. He grabbed my clothes, thrusting them at me.

"Gwyneira, hurry!"

That was when I heard the hammering at the door of the observatory.

"*Brontes, open this door right now!*"

I recognized that voice. My heart dropped to the ground. I fastened my bra and put on my underwear as quickly as I could. I managed to pull my servants' dress over my body and struggled with the buttons when the door to the observatory flew open with a tremendous crash.

Suddenly, the enraged faces of both the king *and* queen glared down at me, barely dressed. Brontes stood between his parents and me—valiantly attempting to shield me from them—but his hands trembled slightly, giving away his hidden panic.

There was a horrible moment of silence. Both his parents scanned their eyes over everything in a bristling, silent outrage.

Their eyes combed over Brontes, who was mostly fully clothed but disheveled. Their judgmental gaze shifted to me with my unbuttoned dress barely hanging onto my shoulders.

Then all hell broke loose.

CHAPTER SEVENTEEN

The king stormed forward at Brontes and slapped him so hard that his lip immediately started to bleed.

The queen set her sights on me. "You disgusting little *harlot*!" She screamed, grabbing a fistful of my hair.

"Let her go, Mother!" As Brontes turned toward us, sparks began to dance off his fists.

But the king slugged him again, knocking him to the ground.

The queen stared at her son, dragging me a few steps forward as she did. "This is completely unacceptable! I was worried about you bringing her to dinner! I didn't think it was *this bad* already!"

"She's my fiancée!" Brontes countered angrily. "Why shouldn't—"

"You idiot!" The king cut him off. "Your engagement is a political ploy to form an alliance with the Ice Kingdom! I thought you knew that?"

The queen threw me to the floor. "We would never actually allow you to marry—let alone breed with—this filthy Ice Enchanted! Her offspring would defile our pure bloodline. She was only ever intended to live here as a servant and be brought out as your fake wife whenever we'd need to show proof of our alliance to the other kingdoms in public. I already arranged for a noble Storm girl to be the actual mother of my grandchildren!"

"No!" I gasped in dismay.

"Shut up! You're ruining everything!" The queen turned to the king. "I told you we should have killed her!"

"We can't kill her," the king replied. "We'll need to prove she's alive to maintain the alliance."

"We can come up with excuses," the queen pondered, ignoring us. "I think we *could* kill her, and no one would notice."

They spoke about my murder as if I were not there.

"You'll do no such thing!" Brontes bellowed, raising himself up.

The king slammed his fists into Brontes' face several times. "Stay down, boy!"

"Stop!" I screamed.

"We'll see, my queen," the king answered. "For now, guards!" A few guards filed in from outside the door.

"Chain this atrocious harlot down in the kitchens, and *do not* let her leave!"

Two of the guards clamped down on my arms and began to drag me away.

"Get your hands off of her!" Brontes pushed himself off the floor, his hands blazing again with furious sparks.

"Seize him too!" The king ordered.

Before Brontes could do anything else, five guards wrestled him down to the floor and tied his hands together.

The king loomed over him. "Take this embarrassment of a prince down to the dungeons and lock him away! I don't want to see him again!"

As Brontes was dragged away, the queen added. "The rest of you—destroy this ridiculous room!"

"NO!" I screamed desperately.

Brontes roared in rage, struggling to free himself from the guards in vain.

Neither of us could stop them. The guards invaded my precious observatory, their swords swinging down on the orrery and smashing it into pieces. Their rampage overturned the bookshelves, shattered the telescopes, and ripped the star maps off the walls.

My stomach dropped seeing *For the Love of Stars: A Study of the Cosmos* sitting helplessly on the map table.

"Please, don't!" I cried and watched in horror as a guard mercilessly hacked away at the table with his sword until it was nothing more than shreds of paper and splinters of wood.

My legs buckled beneath me, powerless as the guards held me in a vice-like grip. My chest heaved with sobs that wouldn't stop. Tears streamed down my face, blurring my vision until everything disappeared in a sea of despair as they wrenched me from the room.

My hands cooled the soapy water as I scrubbed away at the baked-on food. I wasn't sure if it was my ice powers or my tears that cooled the water, but I didn't care.

Every time I moved, the thick shackles around my wrists gave a *clank.* They were so heavy that I couldn't raise my hands up without causing pins and needles. I had to rest them on the wet edge of the sink as I scrubbed continuously.

My eyes ached from how much crying I'd done in the past three days, so swollen I could barely see the dish—only Brontes' distraught face as he screamed, the orrery smashed, and my beloved book destroyed at the end of a sword. Heartbreak sent a sharp pain through my chest as everything good in my life vanished once more.

How could his parents treat their son like this? Despair clouded my thoughts. *Who am I kidding? My parents aren't any better.*

The uncertainty of ever seeing Brontes again weighed heavily on me. Now, chained to the kitchen by shackles around my wrists and ankles, my movements were restricted to a mere five feet—from the dish sink to a small foul-smelling mattress with a chamber pot next to it.

In my previous prison, I found solace in stargazing from the tower, but this basement kitchen offered only windowless walls.

Before, I could roam the castle grounds, visit my observatory, and catch fleeting glimpses of Brontes, despite the queen's efforts to keep us apart. But now, all of that was gone.

No matter how dark things seemed, I desperately tried to find happiness here. But kind people were overshadowed by those with cold hearts and cruel words. A fog of hopelessness began to engulf me as I slowly sank into darkness.

Maybe I should've avoided Brontes like the queen wanted me to. Then this would've never happened. He's better off without me.

A gentle nudge against my arm pulled me from the abyss. Maisol held out a beautifully presented plate of food, as if it had been crafted for the king and queen's dinner.

"Eat something," Maisol said softly. "You really need to."

I shook my head. "No, Maisol. Get away from me—you're going to get in trouble if they see you."

"I don't care," she replied quietly. "You need to eat."

"No, I don't want anyone else being nice to me." Tears dripped off my face.

Suddenly, Rori's sarcastic laugh echoed and drew my attention.

"Well, that's just too bad!" She sneered, placing a goblet on the sink next to me. "Because I've poured some of the good wine for you!"

"You better not let that food go to waste," Dagur scolded. "I personally saw to it that we made a plate for the princess. I don't care if you're not eating at the royal table. You still better eat it."

"Please, everyone," I begged. "The queen will punish all of you."

Rori scoffed. "What is she going to do? Make us servants?"

A chuckle rippled through the group.

"We're going to stand here until you eat," Maisol said firmly. "You're wasting away over here."

"But—"

"Uh-uh." Rori stuck her finger in my face. "Eat!"

Seeing the genuine concern on Maisol, Rori, and Dagur's faces, I conceded, took the plate from Maisol, and brought it to my bed to eat, dragging my restraints behind me.

I timidly took a bite of the roasted duck breast, cooked with onions and carrots, swimming in a creamy white sauce. The flavors ran through my mouth and brought warmth that felt like comfort after so much despair, making me realize how hungry I actually was.

"Thank you, everyone," I murmured.

They really stood there and watched me eat.

"Why are you being so nice to me?" I asked.

Dagur frowned. "Because you're one of us, that's why!"

Maisol and Rori nodded in agreement.

I smiled a little. "Thank you. That means a lot."

As I shoved a few carrots into my mouth, tears welled up in my eyes again, but not tears of sadness—tears of gratitude. I might've been shackled to the kitchen, but I still had my friends. Bronte had no one. Alone in the dungeons, he was now in a much worse prison than my own.

"I just feel so bad for Brontes." I sniffled. "He just wanted to make things better for me, and now he's . . ."

"Yes," Rori agreed solemnly. "I didn't think the prince had it in him to stand up to his parents, but you both proved us all wrong about him."

"Now he's in the dungeon, and it's all my fault!" I wailed.

Maisol fell to her knees to look me in the eye. "It's not. Don't ever think that—it's the king and queen. They are the *only* ones at fault."

Rori and Dagur nodded, and I wiped the saltwater from my raw cheeks.

"I just feel so terrible, Maisol! He doesn't deserve to be there. I'm the one they hate! They're punishing him for caring about me."

Maisol gave me a sad half-smile. "You're not even worried about yourself at all. You really love him, don't you?"

I nodded wistfully. "Of course I do."

"Well, we're just going to have to do something about your situation, won't we?" Rori smirked.

Rori glanced at Maisol, and mischief glinted in both of their eyes.

"Wha-what are you guys talking about?" I asked, trying to contain my hope so I wouldn't be disappointed by the answer.

"Don't worry about it for now." Maisol winked. "Finish your dinner. You're going to need your strength."

"You'll know when the time comes." Rori patted my hand.

As I polished off the rest of my food, my mind raced with possibilities. What could they possibly have in mind? Could they really help me be with Brontes? As much as I wanted to believe Rori and Maisol had something up their sleeve, the doubts plagued me as well. How could Brontes and I possibly be together? The king and queen had made it abundantly clear they would never allow our union, no matter how much I wished it to be true.

But then again, I'd rather have hope than nothing at all.

It was the middle of the night when I heard two people stalking into the kitchen by candlelight. As they approached my bed, I realized it was Maisol and Elias.

"Oh, good, you're awake, Gwyneira," Maisol said. "I brought a friend."

"Hey, Princess." Elias smiled. "I've got a gift for you."

"What's going on?" I asked with confusion.

Elias opened up his palm and produced a key. "Surprise!"

It took me a second to realize the key matched the rusting iron shackles around my wrists and ankles—when I did, my jaw dropped. "But . . . *how?!*"

"I told you those stuck-up bastards treat us like props, but we see *everything*, including where they put the keys!" Elias grinned as he leaned down and inserted the key into the shackle around my ankle. "Maisol said you could use some help, so I'm here, just as I promised!"

As soon as Elias unlocked all my restraints, I threw my arms around him in a tight hug and then hugged Maisol as well.

"Thank you so much!"

"Rori and Dagur helped as well," Maisol noted. "We just didn't want everyone coming back here in the middle of the night to free you."

"Please thank them for me," I said, tenderly rubbing the raw marks on my wrists from the heavy shackles. Though grateful for my newfound freedom, I knew I couldn't enjoy it without Brontes. "But what about Brontes?"

Maisol placed a reassuring hand on my shoulder, her eyes serious and determined. "We have a plan, Gwyn. Many of the guards are sympathetic to you and the prince, and, most of all, they despise the king and queen. They're willing to help."

"Then what?" Panic rose in my chest. "The king and queen will have us both thrown in the dungeon the moment they find us again."

Maisol's gaze flicked over to Elias, who crossed his arms. A faint smile played on his lips. "I will get you two horses from the royal stables so you can flee the castle. The fastest ones we have. You'll be long gone before anyone notices you're missing."

"And go where?" I asked, mostly thinking out loud to myself. "They'll find us if we stay in the Storm Kingdom, and we can't go to the Ice Kingdom. I'm certain my parents would just make us come back here, and I've never been anywhere else."

Elias shrugged. "Beats me. Getting you horses is all I thought through."

"Wait." Maisol's face lit up with an idea. "What about your brother, the Ice Prince?"

"Fannar?"

"Isn't he at Haven Academy? Haven Academy is neutral ground for all the kingdoms. None of your parents could do anything about it if you went there."

Elias nodded eagerly in agreement.

The mention of my brother stirred a warmth in my chest. Outside of the Storm Castle, he's the only person I could trust. It was perfect. "Yes, Fannar will help us. He always has."

"Then it's settled," Elias declared, determination etched on his face. "You and Brontes will head to Haven Academy after escaping the castle."

"Sounds like a plan." Maisol grinned.

I bit nervously at my lower lip, my heart pounding with equal parts apprehension and hope. Could we really pull this off? My brows knit together, and fear clouded my thoughts. "What if something goes wrong? What if we're caught? I don't want all of you to be punished for helping us."

"What will they do? Throw us in the dungeon? We'll be out in a few hours once they realize they need someone to clean the horse crap!" Elias confidently chuckled.

Maisol clasped my hand in hers, offering me a gentle smile. "You know the ins and outs of the castle, Gwyn. You can do this."

"Remember, you're one of us." Elias grinned. "You have friends everywhere."

I nodded.

"Time to get that prince of yours out of the dungeon." Maisol stood up.

"Now?" My eyes lit up with excitement.

"Now." Elias nodded. "We've already spoken to the dungeon guards assigned to his cell. They will provide you with the key, but other guards loyal to the king and queen are patrolling as well. Do your best to stay hidden, but if you do come across someone, say, 'The storm is coming.' If they're on our side, they'll respond with 'Let the storm break.'"

"Got it." I nodded, committing the secret code to memory.

"Once you get the prince, take him to the servants' quarters," Maisol instructed. "Elias will meet you there with the horses. If anything goes wrong, just come back to the servants' quarters. We'll figure out what to do next."

With the plan solidified, I took a deep breath as the weight of responsibility began to sink in, bracing myself for the challenge ahead. But the thought of reuniting with Fannar and, more importantly, running away with Brontes filled me with a sense of clarity and purpose, like a spark had been lit from within.

A surge of gratitude for their kindness and friendship filled my heart. "I don't know how to thank you all!"

"Well, not getting caught would be a good start." Elias smirked.

"Thank you for everything." My voice wavered with emotion as I spoke. The fear still lingered, but knowing I wasn't alone gave me strength.

Maisol gave me one last hug. "Now, go!" she hissed.

I nodded and ran from the kitchen as fast as my legs could carry me. As I darted through the dimly lit corridors of the castle, my heart hammered with nerves, but they couldn't quell the fervor burning within. Brontes needed me. I would do anything to be with him, even if it meant fleeing into the unknown together.

Brontes, I thought. *I'm coming.*

Once he was free, we would ride like the wind was chasing us. Toward freedom, toward a future that was ours to shape.

"The storm is coming," I murmured under my breath.

I am the storm.

CHAPTER EIGHTEEN

My heart raced as I slipped through the dark halls, trying to remain unseen in the still early morning hours before daylight. The dungeon lay at the other end of the Storm Castle. Every creak of the floorboards beneath me felt like a shout, announcing my presence to the entire castle.

As I tiptoed past lavish tapestries that adorned the walls, thoughts of Brontes consumed me. Images of his fierce eyes and strong yet gentle touch filled my mind, distracting me from the fear that gnawed at my insides. My stomach twisted with anxiety, not only from the danger of sneaking around the castle but also from the anticipation of seeing him again.

As I turned a corner, I nearly collided with a housekeeper, her arms laden with linens.

"Your Highness." She looked up in surprise, her eyes widening as she recognized me. Her name escaped me, but I'd seen her face in passing. "What are you doing here?"

"The storm is coming," I whispered, hoping she was an ally.

She held a finger to her lips and nodded. "Let the storm break." Her words offered me a small measure of assurance as she continued down the hall, leaving me to continue my journey undisturbed.

I need to be more careful.

Once I reached the entrance to the dungeons, I hesitated for a moment, taking a deep breath to steady myself, before I descended into the darkness.

The air grew oppressively warm as I crept my way down the stone steps. Torches flickered along the walls, casting eerie shadows that danced along the rough surfaces. The stench of sewage and rusted metal assaulted my senses. My stomach churned in disgust as I thought of Brontes being imprisoned here for the last three days.

When I reached the stairway landing, I pressed myself against the wall, hiding in the shadows, before slowly peering over the half-wall of the stairs to survey the scene beneath me.

The long, narrow dungeon corridor stretched out ahead, rows of prison cells lining both sides. Most contained castle servants, slumped down, appearing dejected and despondent. The heavy stone walls enclosed individual cells, each housing a single prisoner. Iron bars secured the entrances with locked doors. The walls between the cells stood at a height of ten feet, while the ceiling extended an additional six feet above. Despite its quaint and antiquated appearance, minerals that greatly suppressed Enchanted powers fortified the stone and iron of the cells, while still permitting the dungeon guards to utilize their own abilities when necessary. Four guards were stationed throughout the space, their swords glinting in the dim light.

Brontes, where are you? I wondered, my breath catching in my throat as anxiety clawed at my insides. *What do I do now?*

It would've been impossible to use the path between the cells without being seen by the guards. I couldn't risk being spotted out in the open. A plan began to form in my mind, as reckless as it was necessary. If I couldn't walk between the cells, perhaps I could find another way.

My heart pounded in my chest as I summoned the cold from within and pressed my hands on the edge of the stairway's half-wall. An elevated platform of ice began to extend from it, parallel to the corridor below, but high enough to walk above the cells.

A calming cold seeped through my tattered shoes as I took my first hesitant steps across the ice, careful not to slip or make any noise that would alert the guards below.

As I passed over the cells, some prisoners below glanced up at me, their eyes wide with surprise or curiosity, but none dared to betray me.

As I approached the end of the corridor, my gaze fell on Brontes, lying asleep on the cold stone floor of his cell. Bruises and cuts marred his face and forearms, evidence of the beatings he'd endured since being thrown into the dungeon.

"Brontes," I whispered to myself, tears pricking at the corners of my eyes. A wave of protectiveness washed over me, anger simmering beneath the surface at the sight of his injuries. How could his own parents let someone do this to him? He was the strongest person I knew, but seeing him so vulnerable, so broken, shattered something inside me.

My prince.

As I continued to watch him, his chest rose and fell with each breath, and I found myself holding mine in response. I wanted so much to jump down and touch him, to assure myself that he was really there, that he was still alive despite the cruelty inflicted upon him.

But I couldn't. Not yet.

The icy platform shuttered beneath me as my emotions threatened to overwhelm me, teetering on the edge of control. I took another step, but this time, I lost my footing on the slick ice. The thud as I collapsed echoed through the stone walls.

"What was that?" one of the guards asked, peering into the dimness.

My heart dropped. Goosebumps rippled up and down my skin. I bit my lip and cringed silently, certain I'd been caught.

"Your wretched king and queen are nothing but tyrants!" a voice boomed from a distant cell. "They'll get what's coming to them! Just you wait!"

"Long live the true rulers of this kingdom!" another prisoner chimed in with a maniacal laugh.

"Silence!" the guard barked, his attention now on the prisoners' outbursts.

More voices joined the cacophony of insults and threats.

"Down with the false monarchs! May they rot in these dungeons themselves!" someone shouted.

"Death to the imposters!" One of the prisoners closer to me hollered before looking up and winking at me.

Thank you, I mouthed silently.

"Rid us of their tyranny!" another added with glee.

"Down with the king and queen!" yelled yet another.

"Silence!" the guard ordered.

As the chaos grew louder, two of the guards grumbled and left to deal with the obnoxious prisoners, leaving only two behind in front of Brontes' cell.

The commotion had awakened Brontes, his eyes widening as he noticed me perched above him on the ice bridge. A mix of surprise and concern painted his face, his eyebrows furrowing together as his gaze scanned the scene for any threat. I pressed a finger to my lips, urging him to stay silent.

The two remaining guards seemed unmoved by the chaos around us, standing like statues before Brontes' cell. Elias said they were on our side, yet fear still gripped me, doubting their allegiance to our cause. But there was no turning back now.

"The storm is coming," I whispered just loud enough for them to hear me.

The guards glanced up at me, then exchanged a knowing look between them.

"Ludvik," one guard said to the other. "We better check on the other guards."

"Yes, Cid," Ludvik agreed. "It sounds like a lot of the prisoners are worked up. We don't want a riot on our hands."

Cid crouched down, placing a key quietly on the ground with deliberate care. He looked up at me to make sure I noticed it.

I nodded.

"Let the storm break," they both uttered under their breaths before walking away from Brontes' cell, leaving him unattended.

Relief flooded through me, but I knew we weren't safe yet. As soon as the coast was clear, I hopped down from the ice bridge, my feet hitting the stone floor with a soft thud. My hands snatched the key off the ground, my heart racing as I rushed to unlock the cell door.

"Gwyneira!" Brontes exclaimed. "How did you—?"

"My friends in the castle staff!" I answered quickly as I shoved the key into the lock. "We're getting out of here tonight."

The door to his cell unlocked with a satisfying click. I flung it open before running straight into Brontes' open arms.

He pulled me in close, his big, strong arms encircling my shoulders in a fierce hug. "I'm so glad you're okay," he whispered.

I leaned back from his embrace and placed my hand on his bruised cheek. "Your poor face."

"I'll be fine."

My body tensed at the sound of footsteps, interrupting the reverie of our reunion.

"We need to go!" I urged. "They'll be back soon."

Heart thumping in my chest, Brontes and I moved cautiously through the dimly lit dungeon with our fingers intertwined as we navigated the shadows.

"Wait," Brontes whispered, stopping abruptly. I held my breath, straining to hear any sign of approaching guards. A cacophony of heavy boots echoed down the corridor, making my heart race even faster.

"Here!" I pulled Brontes into a shadowy alcove. We pressed ourselves against the cold, damp wall as several more guards appeared, searching the area with fierce determination.

"The prince has escaped!" a guard called out to the others.

"Find him!" another barked, frustration dripping from every word.

"He can't be far!" the first guard hissed. "The king and queen will have our heads if we don't find him!"

As soon as they marched past us, we crept into the corridor and headed toward the dungeon's exit.

"Stop, Your Highness!" A guard suddenly appeared in front of us, sword in hand, with four more guards behind him.

I whirled around to see four more guards blocking our retreat. *Shit.*

Cid and Ludvik emerged from the shadows, clutching their weapons tightly.

"Stand down, Your Highnesses!" Ludvik ordered. "There is nowhere left to run."

The guards closed in tighter around us.

"Good work!" A knight, who appeared to be the captain, grumbled, ominously moving toward us. "Apprehend them both!"

Panic rose in my chest as my gaze shifted to Brontes. He had a look I'd never seen before. A dark one. His eyes flashed with rage, and energy crackled around his hands, ready to defend us.

This was it. I turned to face the guards behind us, spreading out my arms and readying myself to summon the most powerful ice storm I could muster. Frost began to form on my hands. We weren't going down without a fight.

Suddenly, Cid stepped forward, raising his hand.

"Wait," he told the captain. "The storm is coming."

At his words, all but two of the guards stiffened and shouted in unison. "Let the storm break!"

They turned their swords toward the captain and the one remaining guard.

"Wh-what are you doing?" the captain stammered, his face a mask of confusion and fear.

"Protecting our prince and princess," Ludvik replied coolly, leveling his weapon at him.

"Long live, King Brontes!" Cid shouted.

"Long live, King Brontes!" the other guards repeated.

"Go!" Ludvik urged us.

"Thank you," Brontes said, marveling at the bravery of those who had banded together for us. "Your loyalty will never be forgotten."

"Thank you," I whispered to Cid and Ludvik with gratitude. They simply nodded, their eyes full of pride.

Brontes and I reached the lush lawn in front of the servants' quarters to find nearly all the castle staff congregated there.

"You did it!" Rori exclaimed as soon as she saw us.

The servants erupted into applause and hollers. When I glanced at Brontes, his back was as straight as a board. His eyes scanned the crowd with a look of disbelief.

"Are the horses ready?" Maisol called out.

"Yes, they're ready to go!" Elias nodded.

"Let's get you two out of here!" Rori grabbed my shoulders, ready to say goodbye.

"Wait," Brontes said suddenly.

The sound of his voice was calm and quiet, yet it seemed to reverberate through the air, and a hush fell over the crowd. In that moment of stillness, all eyes drifted toward me since no one knew what to do next.

"What it is, Brontes?" I asked.

He surveyed the staff gathered before us with a heavy heart. "Most of the prisoners in the dungeons were castle staff because they angered my parents in some way. One girl was there for something as trivial as spilling tea on my mother! What's going to happen to everyone here once my parents realize they helped us escape? There will be hell to pay."

The silence lingered until Maisol spoke up bravely, "We can handle it."

A murmur of agreement swept through the crowd as heads nodded.

"No," Brontes turned to them. "I won't have any more of you thrown into the dungeons. Gods know that I've put you all through enough."

The servants gaped at each other, astonished. Even I was taken aback.

"I'm sorry," Brontes continued, his voice loud and confident as he addressed the assembled people. "I'm sorry to each one of you that I've yelled at, sorry for knocking things out of your hands, sorry for every time you had to refurnish my room, sorry for scaring you, and . . . I'm just sorry for my attitude."

I smiled, so proud of Brontes for opening up to the servants.

"Thank you for saving the most precious person in my life," Brontes looked at me. "My Gwyneira."

I stepped beside him and intertwined my hand in his. He continued, "You and Gwyneira have shown me what it means to be brave and have inspired me to stand up for what I believe, no matter the consequences. I'm done trying to become the prince they want me to be. It's time for me to be the *king* who does what is right. I'm going to overthrow my parents."

Gasps spread through the crowd at Brontes' treasonous words. But my heart swelled with pride. This was the man I was to marry—strong and just, who would not shy away from standing up to his own family to defend others.

"Brontes." I squeezed his hand. "You won't have to face them alone. I stand with you."

"How, Your Highness?" Rori asked.

"Since my parents banned the use of powers, they've neglected their powers for far too long, allowing them to grow weak." He smiled at me. "Meanwhile, Gwyneira and I have been practicing. If they do not agree to step down, we will take the throne by force."

"But how far are you willing to go, Your Highness?" Maisol asked, her brow furrowed with skepticism.

My heart clenched at her question, but I knew it must be asked. Brontes needed to face the possible consequences of this decision.

"I will do whatever must be done," Brontes replied without hesitation. "Even if it means throwing my own parents in the dungeon . . . or worse. I hope they will agree without a fight, but I can't let things return to the way they were before."

His gaze swept over the gathered crowd before continuing, "I won't leave you to face their wrath alone. My responsibility is to protect this kingdom, and that includes all of you." He paused to give me a fierce look. "And my Princess Gwyneira. I swear, I will fight for all of you."

The unwavering conviction in his voice rattled me to my core.

Maisol's voice rang out, strong and steady. "Then I stand with you, Your Highness."

"Me too." Rori stepped forward.

"Same here!" Elias thumped a fist against his chest.

A young servant's voice rose from the back of the gathered crowd.

"Me too!" he called out, and the words were echoed back in a delirious chorus of affirmations. A wave of energy charged through the air, a mix of excitement and nervous anticipation.

"Now what, Your Highness?" Dagur's question cut through the noise.

Brontes paused as the crowd grew quiet again. "I think Gwyneira and I should confront my parents alone first—we'll see if they're willing to go peacefully."

"And if not?" Rori chimed in, punching one hand into her other palm.

"Then we'll need backup," Brontes replied, his jaw set with determination. "We need all the allies we can get."

"Dagur and I will free the prisoners in the dungeons," Elias said, a fire in his eyes, and Dagur nodded once.

"Rori and I can gather the rest of the castle staff who are on our side," Maisol added. "We'll be ready to back you up if a fight breaks out."

"Perfect, we need as much support as possible." Brontes nodded. "Meet us outside of the king and queen's chambers, and be ready if a fight breaks out." He turned to the crowd. "Everyone, we must be ready for whatever this brings. Be brave, be strong, and remember, we're fighting for a better kingdom."

Elias yelled with unbridled fury, "The storm is coming!" His battle cry echoed across the castle grounds as he raised his clenched fist to the heavens.

The spark of hope and resolve ignited in the eyes of everyone around us.

"Let the storm break!" the servants roared in response. Their unified voices merged into an unstoppable force that could have shaken the very foundations of the castle.

As the crowd dispersed, my stomach fluttered with excitement, but it also tightened into a hard knot of anticipation, apprehension mounting with every breath. My heart constricted as I realized there was no turning back now.

Brontes smiled at me, his strong, calloused fingers wrapping gently around mine. "Ready, snowflake?"

"Ready." I nodded.

With our hearts pounding and our fate uncertain, Brontes and I turned toward the castle, hand in hand. One way or another, everything would change.

CHAPTER NINETEEN

"Are you sure you want to do this?" I squeezed his hand as we ascended the spiral staircase toward the king and queen's chambers.

Brontes gave a dry laugh. "No, but I don't think I have a choice anymore."

"Do you know what you're going to say?"

"No, I don't. It's weird. I've thought about this day for so long, but now, I'm at a loss for words." He shook his head, his brow furrowed.

"You've stood up to them before. You can do it again."

Brontes took an uneasy breath. "I know." He pulled my hand to lips and kissed my knuckles. "As long as you're with me."

"Every step of the way." I smiled softly. "Whatever happens, I'm so proud of you."

We reached the doors of his parents' chambers, and he gave me a melancholic smile.

"Thanks for standing by me, Gwyneira. I couldn't have done this without you. I love you, my snowflake." The glow in his eyes warmed my soul.

"I love you too, my prince."

Our lips came together in a brief and tender kiss.

"Alright." He held his fist over the door. "Let's do this."

I nodded.

Brontes knocked on the door. Such a polite way to start a coup.

"Come in," said the Storm King's voice from behind the doors.

Brontes pushed open the grand doors to the royal chambers. I followed him in, stepping into the king and queen's opulent bedroom for the first time.

Dark-colored frescoes of storm clouds adorned the high-arched ceiling, and grand tapestries clung to the walls, spinning tales of epic battles and mythical heroes. The furniture, constructed from deep, glossy wood, shone with gilded accents and intricate engravings. Thick, plush purple carpets blanketed the floors. Velvet drapery framed large windows as warm, golden light danced across the room from the flaming candelabras. The magnificent four-poster bed swathed in luxurious linens and elegantly embroidered pillows filled the room with decadent artistry. A large fireplace snapped and hissed with flames.

The king had settled into an ornate armchair, one hand clasped around a cup of steaming tea, the other holding open a book. The queen sat in front of a bejeweled antique vanity, its surface lined with crystal bottles and jars. A silver brush moved slowly through her satin black hair, each stroke sending ripples across the shiny mirror.

Their eyes widened with surprise at our impromptu entrance.

"Brontes!" the Storm King snapped. "How did you escape?!"

"What is that atrocious girl doing here?" The Storm Queen's face contorted in disgust. She turned her head toward the door and shouted, "Guards!"

"No!" Brontes commanded. "This time, you'll listen to me! You will listen or face the consequences."

His parents froze, looking at him incredulously.

"During my time in the dungeons, I've seen firsthand how cruel you are," Brontes continued. "Not just to me, but to everyone—the castle staff and, of course, Gwyneira. I won't tolerate it any longer."

He paused to glare at them with his fists clenched. "I'm giving you one chance to step down from the throne."

The king and queen threw back their heads in laughter, exchanging smug glances at each other. The sound of their contemptuous cackles echoed through the chambers.

"Our dear little boy thinks he can tell us what to do," the king sneered.

"Oh, Brontes." The Storm Queen's eyes jabbed him with mockery. "You're still such a child."

"Enough!" Brontes shouted without a falter as his powers crackled around him, sparks dancing across his skin.

His parents' laughter died immediately, replaced by glints of fear in their eyes. It was unmistakable now.

"I wasn't sure if I saw it before, but now I'm certain," I piped up, gazing thoughtfully at the king and queen. "You're both afraid of him."

"Because he's dangerous!" his mother spat. "He's a monster. He can't control his powers!"

"No!" Brontes' hands glowed brighter as he raised them toward the ceiling. A rumble of thunder shook the room, and a cluster of dark clouds formed above us.

The queen scuttled into a corner, her eyes wide with shock. Even the king stepped back, his face pale.

"I can control my powers just fine. You told me that my Combined Enchanted mark meant I was dangerous, but that's not what it means, is it? You're afraid because you can no longer control *me*." A sudden realization washed over his face, as if a puzzle piece finally clicked into place. "You banned powers from the court because you're afraid of how strong I'd become. It was never to protect our people. It was to prevent me from learning to use my powers so you could continue to control me."

"Your mark is proof that you're an abomination!" the queen snarled. "Our bloodline is pure Storm Enchanted, and yet you are a Combined Enchanted!"

"And to be tainted with pitiful ice no less!" the king sneered. "The ice in your blood has already poisoned your mind, boy! Falling for this damn Ice girl, as if you weren't an utter disappointment of a prince already."

"This is all your fault!" The queen's voice shook with fury, her eyes blazing as she glowered at me. "You've corrupted my son. You'll pay for this!"

She hurled a lightning bolt at me, but Brontes was quicker. With a flick of his wrist, he deflected it with a bolt of his own.

"Leave her alone!" he growled. His eyes narrowed dangerously as he stood squarely between me and his mother. "Gwyneira has done nothing but try to please you since she got here. Isn't it funny, Mother and Father? The fiancée you arranged for me to marry but are now unwilling to accept is the one who made me realize your failures."

"Bold words from such a weak prince," the king sneered from across the room, his fists sparking with electric energy. "A vile Combined Enchanted like you dare to usurp us?"

"Father, I don't want to fight you," Brontes replied, clenching his fists, electricity crackling around them. "But I will if I must."

"Then you must be punished!" the king roared, lunging at his son. A flash of lightning shot through the air, striking Brontes and sending him crashing into a nearby table.

"Brontes!" I screamed, ice flaring in my hands.

"I'm fine, Gwyneira. Let me handle this." Brontes rose, gritting his teeth against the pain. "Is this how it's going to be then?" he retorted, launching himself toward his father.

Bolts of electricity arced between the two, streaking through the air and raining sparks around them. The flashes of bright white and yellow light were almost blinding as they shot across the room. The walls trembled from the impact, competing with the sound of clashing thunderous energies.

"Enough is enough!" the queen screeched, raising her hands to the heavens. A fierce, swirling whirlpool of dark clouds descended upon us. Books, picture frames, and other objects spun violently, hitting the walls and breaking into pieces. Debris flew around the air in a wild frenzy, creating a smoke-filled haze.

Running quickly to Brontes' side, I encased us with a translucent dome of shimmering blue-white ice, shielding us from the chaos. The barrier protected us in a pocket of safety, its curved edges repelling flying debris. But it wasn't enough. Brontes knew it too, eyeing the cracks forming in the ice.

His hands curled into fists, and sparks of electricity crackled around them again. Chunks of hail descended from the ceiling, pelting his parents mercilessly in a relentless barrage as they tried to run for cover.

"This ends now!" Brontes bellowed before conjuring his own monstrous tornado that filled the entire room.

The cyclone slammed his parents against the wall. As they hung there, dazed and disoriented, I seized the opportunity to freeze their bodies in place.

"Mother, Father," Brontes panted, the exhaustion of battle etched into his face. "This is your final warning. I'm requesting your respect for Gwyneira as the future queen and your peaceful surrender."

His parents remained silent, their faces stony, unyielding, and filled with animosity.

"Very well," Brontes said, his eyes narrowing. "I didn't want it to come to this, but if you won't surrender willingly, I have no choice but to imprison you in the dungeon until you're ready for a peaceful discussion."

The words of his final plea for reason hung heavy in the air like an oppressive fog. His chest rose and fell with each weighted, sorrowful breath as he grappled with the heartbreaking decision.

"Your Highness!" Maisol burst into the disheveled room, flanked by a group of castle staff. Brontes turned to look at them. Their faces were resolute with loyalty to their prince. My heart surged with gratitude for their support. "We're here to stand with you!"

"What is the meaning of this?!" The king's face contorted with rage, struggling against the ice that held him against the wall.

"It's a coup, Father," Brontes replied simply. "The people have spoken, and they are willing to fight if they must."

"Preposterous!" the queen snapped, her eyes narrowing. "This is treason! You cannot possibly believe that this . . . this *farce* will succeed. Traitors, all of you!" She glared at Brontes. "How could you do this to us?!"

As Brontes turned to answer her, I caught a dangerous glint in the king's eye. Faint sparks fizzed around him, and

I knew without a doubt he intended to strike Brontes once more. Something within me responded.

It started as a pit in my stomach—a mix of fear and anger that he wanted to hurt my Brontes. The rage boiled into an uncontrollable energy that surged throughout my body. A thousand synapses fired up and down my body in a chain reaction of sparks. My hands trembled as the anger-infused pressure built up inside me. It demanded to be released.

"No!" The word thundered out of me like a freight train as I forced my open hand forward.

CHAPTER TWENTY

The roar of power coursing through my body erupted from my fingertips, leaving the slightest tingle along my arm in its wake. A blinding blue-white burst of lightning surged toward the king, striking him before he could hurt Brontes.

Gasps filled the room and then fell silent as everyone stared at me. I peered down at my quivering hands, in shock at what I'd just done. My body still tingled with an exhilarating thrill as the wild, untamed energy vibrated through me, yet somehow, it also felt familiar, like a missing part of me had been found.

"Gwyneira!" Brontes' eyes sparkled with admiration and amazement. He pointed toward my right shoulder. "You're . . . glowing."

Glancing down, the Combined Enchanted mark on my right collarbone gave off a white ethereal light before fading away a few seconds later.

"Impossible!" the queen sneered. "How did you—"

"That's right, Mother," Brontes scoffed at her. "Did I forget to mention that she's also a 'vile' Combined Enchanted too?"

"By the gods, Gwyneira!" Maisol exclaimed, her eyes wide. "You truly are fated to be the queen of the Storm Kingdom."

As if on cue, the gathered servants erupted into cheers, their voices filled with hope and determination. Brontes glanced at me with pride, and his hand intertwined with mine.

"Guards, since my parents obviously will not surrender willingly, please take them to the dungeon," Brontes commanded.

"Yes, Storm King," one of the guards responded.

"King?" Brontes' eyebrows furrowed in confusion.

Maisol smiled.

Rori laughed, emerging from behind Maisol. "The king and queen can't fulfill their duties in the royal dungeons. That makes their heir the new king, Your Majesty!"

"Yes, I guess you're right." Brontes stared at his parents, the weight of disappointment heavy in his gaze. His eyes shimmered with unshed tears as he slowly shifted away from them. "This wasn't the way I wanted it to happen," he whispered to himself.

My heart ached for him, and I squeezed his hand, not knowing what to say.

As the guards led Brontes' parents away, the castle staff erupted into cheers of "King Brontes!" and "Long live the king!" Their excitement resounded off the walls.

Brontes collected himself and stepped into the hallway outside of the royal chambers where they gathered. "Thank you for your faith in us." His voice was confident and assertive. "From now on, things will change for the better. Together, we will build a brighter future for our kingdom!"

"The storm is coming!" someone shouted.

"Let the storm break!" The crowd roared their approval, each cheer filling the air with hope.

As Brontes pulled me into an embrace, their voices melded together as they chanted even louder, "Long live King Brontes! Long live Queen Gwyneira!"

As my name echoed in the chorus of loyalty and confidence, attached to the title "queen," a strange mix of pride and responsibility washed over me. Though it took me by surprise, one thing was undeniable. I finally found where I belonged.

A few hours later, Brontes and I returned to his room, the door closing behind us with a definitive click. The weight of the morning's events had taken their toll on him. Exhaustion and sleep deprivation had sapped the color from his face, leaving it gaunt and pale. His lips sagged into a loose frown, and his shoulders slumped heavily in weariness. Deep shadows lurked beneath his tired, red-rimmed eyes as they stared out into the distance. It was impossible to tell if he was ruminating on what had happened or if fatigue rendered him unable to process anything at all.

"Brontes," I began gently, placing a hand on his arm. "It must've been hard for you to send your parents to the dungeon."

He sighed heavily, running a hand through his tousled hair. "I really didn't want to, but they left me no choice. They were out of control."

"I know," I said softly, urging him to meet my gaze. "You did the right thing, and you stood up for what was best for our kingdom. I'm so proud of you."

A ghost of a smile flickered across his face. "Thank you, Gwyneira."

"Maybe one day," I ventured, my fingers tracing patterns on his arm. "They'll come around and understand that you're doing this for the good of the kingdom."

"I hope so." His eyes clouded over again, and his brows knitted together. "But I won't hold my breath."

"Whatever happens . . ." I pulled him closer, cupping his face in my hand. "We'll face it together. You're not alone. You'll *never* be alone."

His strong arms encircled me in a tight embrace. "Thank you, my snowflake. That means more to me than you could ever know."

"Me too," I whispered, resting my head on his chest, finding comfort in the sound of his heartbeat.

The late evening air carried the sweet aroma of baked goods as I stood by Maisol's side in the warm kitchen. It'd been a few weeks since Brontes became king. Though I no longer lived my life as a servant, I still found comfort in helping Maisol with her culinary creations. That night, she made cherry turnovers for breakfast tomorrow, and fortunately, she didn't ask me to pit the cherries this time.

"Your Highness, would you mind passing me the sugar?" Maisol asked, her voice perfectly respectful as others bustled around us.

Out of respect for my standing as future queen, Maisol only called me by my name when we were alone or out of earshot from the others.

"Of course," I replied, reaching for the glass jar on the counter.

As she whisked the sugar into the bowl, this bustling kitchen oddly provided me with a sense of familiarity I couldn't find in many places. Moments like these made me treasure my friendship with Maisol even more.

"Can I do anything else to help?" I asked, eager to be of use.

Maisol chuckled softly, her eyes crinkling at the corners. "Honestly, just your company is enough, Your Highness. It means a lot that you come down here, even though you don't have to anymore."

"I can't believe you still come down here, Your Highness!" Rori shouted from in front of the sink. "You wouldn't see me near this place if I didn't have to be here!"

I laughed. "I just can't stay away from you and Maisol."

The kitchen door swung open, and Brontes strode in. The staff stopped what they were doing to bow.

"Your Majesty," the servants acknowledged him.

"Please ignore me and continue what you're doing." He nodded politely.

His eyes scanned the space until they found me. A hint of amusement danced in his gaze as he approached Maisol and me.

"Princess," he greeted with a slight bow and teasing tone in his voice. "How did I know I'd find you here?" His eyes flicked to Maisol, who struggled to suppress a grin. "I hope she's not causing you any trouble."

"Your Majesty," she replied. "I've informed her numerous times that she's no longer a servant, but Her Royal Highness is always welcome here . . . even if her talents lie elsewhere."

A flush crept up my cheeks as I crossed my arms defensively. "I help," I insisted, even though I knew my culinary skills left much to be desired.

"Of course, Gwyneira," Brontes said, barely containing his laughter. "I'm sure your presence alone adds a touch of magic to every dish."

Maisol snickered, "More like a touch of ice!"

I pouted, feeling outnumbered in their playful jests.

Brontes' smile softened, and he reached out to take my hand. "Come, my princess. There's something I want to show you."

He led me out of the kitchen and into the palace gardens, the warm evening air caressing my skin as we walked.

"What's going on?" I asked with curiosity and anticipation.

"You'll see," he replied without saying more.

The garden was bathed in the soft glow of lanterns, casting shadows that danced along the cobblestone paths.

We arrived at the secluded alcove, nestled under a canopy of blooming roses and surrounded by flowering vines. The same special place where, months ago, Brontes had first given me *For the Love of Stars: A Study of the Cosmos.*

"Please have a seat, milady." He gestured to the stone bench at the center of the alcove.

As I lowered myself on to the bench, I glanced around with a mixture of nostalgia and longing. It felt like a lifetime ago since that day, before the observatory had been destroyed and my precious book along with it.

Brontes reached under the bench and pulled out a large gift black box, presenting it to me with a flourish. "I thought you might like this."

My lips curved into an excited smile as I carefully opened the box, revealing its contents.

Inside, the gilded words *For the Love of Stars: A Study of the Cosmos* gleamed back at me. My beloved book, much more worn than before, as if it had been through another ten years of history, but still fully intact. Tears welled up in my eyes as I traced my fingers over its familiar cover.

"How is this possible?" I breathed, overwhelmed by the unexpected reunion with my cherished possession. "I saw them destroy it."

"You saw them destroy the table." Brontes rubbed my back gently. "But the book made it. The housekeepers found it while cleaning the remains of the observatory."

"Thank you," I whispered, clutching the book to my chest. Joy and gratitude swirled within me, making it hard to find the right words to express just how much this gift meant to me.

Brontes put his arm around my shoulders, drawing me close. Enveloped by the fragrance of roses and the soft rustle of leaves, I didn't think I could be any happier.

"Now that things have settled down in the kingdom," Brontes began, his voice steady and thoughtful. "I've been thinking about your future, Gwyneira."

My head snapped up at him, my fingers tightening around the worn cover of the book. What did he mean by "my future"? Not *our* future?

"I've truly appreciated your support during my transition to the throne, but I know it's always been your dream to go to the academy with your brother." Brontes' gaze searched mine. "I can manage here on my own. Do you want to attend Haven Academy with Fannar?"

My stomach sank, my heart twisted, and my fists clenched around the book even tighter, almost of their own accord. Heat swept over my cheeks. With a tight jaw and quivering voice, I blurted out, “So you don’t want to marry me anymore?”

Brontes’ eyes widened, and he quickly shook his head. “No! Oh, my gods, Gwyneira! That’s not what I meant at all.” He grasped my hand to reassure me. “I just . . . honestly, I don’t know what I would do without you. But I don’t want you to give up on your dream because of me.”

Tears welled up in the corners of my eyes as I realized how deeply he cared for me, being willing to let me go if it meant fulfilling my dreams. My hand squeezed his tightly. “Brontes, my dreams have changed. I want to stay by your side, as long as you’ll have me.”

“Are you sure?” He brushed the back of his fingers tenderly along my cheek. “I’ll still be here when you graduate.”

“I’m sure.” I elbowed him. “Plus, you need me.”

“That I do.” He let out a slight laugh as he rose from the bench and offered me his hand. “Come on. I’ve got one more surprise for you.” As I took his hand, he pulled me up playfully. “Hurry! We need to go quickly!”

“What?” I giggled. “Why the rush all of a sudden?”

"There's something special happening with the stars tonight!" He dragged me hastily out of the garden. "We need to see it."

"I know, Brontes!" I protested, noticing we were heading toward the field on the side of the castle. "Dereus and Aztos are going to be visible tonight, but I'm going to need my telescope to see them!"

Brontes stopped in his tracks for a moment, then gave a small, sheepish laugh before continuing to lead me forward. "Yeah, okay, but I'm not talking about that! I'm talking about something else! Come on! Come on!"

When we arrived at the field, thick black clouds drenched the sky in darkness. A storm must have rolled in after dinner.

My fingers pressed against my lips. "Oh, no! We won't be able to see anything in the sky at all!"

"I'm sure it'll pass soon." He tilted my chin up gently and lifted my gaze to meet his.

Those deep navy blues spread out before me, speckled with flecks of gray and silver when they caught the moonlight. They transfixed me in much the same way as staring into the night sky did.

"Do you remember when you first brought me out here to use my powers?" he asked.

I nodded, still lost in his beautiful gaze.

A cheeky smile spread across his face. "And we kissed in the rain?"

"Of course!" I giggled, covering my face shyly.

"Gwyneira . . ." When I glanced back up at him, he gave a soft smile. "Being out here with you was the happiest moment of my life up until that moment. Before that, I was so miserable all the time. My powers were tearing me apart from the inside."

"Brontes," I whispered wistfully.

"But," he emphasized, "after you arrived, my life got better in ways I never could've imagined. Everyone's did. You're like a ray of sunshine, clearing out the dark gloom over the entire place."

Warmth snuck into my cheeks from his flattering words.

"I felt something special when I first laid eyes on you, you know," he continued. "And I don't mean just in my pants, though I felt it there too." He smirked coyly.

"Brontes!" I laughed and playfully smacked his chest.

"Okay, seriously." His big grin softened into a light smile. "I knew you were special from the moment I first laid eyes on you. From the day we met, our path has never been easy . . . or normal for that matter, not even for an arranged marriage."

I smiled softly.

"I know we never asked for this. You never asked for me," he continued. "But it felt like we're two halves of the same storm—you never showed emotions and I couldn't control mine—like we were meant for each other. And it was that evening in this field when I knew it for sure."

"Knew what?" I slanted my head curiously.

"That I never want to be without you."

I gazed into his sparkling navy eyes with a huge grin.

He suddenly looked up at the sky, "Oh, would you look at that? The sky is clearing up."

I tilted my head upward, and the thick dark clouds parted to reveal a patch of star-filled night sky, framed by the velvety darkness. A cascade of shining chunks of hail floated over us, like diamonds reflecting the starlight. Each one had been perfectly arranged to spell out an enchanting message: *Will you marry me?*

I gasped and my head snapped back to Brontes. He knelt down in front of me on the damp grass, his hands cupped together and holding a little black velvet box. He opened it slowly before presenting it with outstretched hands, revealing a glimmering ring inside.

"Will you marry me, Gwyneira?" he asked.

CHAPTER TWENTY-ONE

"Brontes . . ." I breathed for a second, then broke down into giggles. "But I thought we're already engaged!"

Brontes chuckled too, still on one knee. "I know, but that doesn't count!"

"Well, I thought it counted," I teased him, unable to stop the grin that blossomed on my face.

He then smiled softly. "We didn't know each other, and we weren't given a choice. But after that night, I knew that even if I could have any girl in the entire kingdom, it was you that I wanted to spend the rest of my life with. I want you to have a choice, not just because our parents decided it for us."

The heat in my cheeks grew warmer in delight.

"But I guess you're right." He chuckled again, a glint of mischief in his eyes. "Maybe I should change the question." He waved his hand in a sweeping motion over his head, and when I looked up again, the constellation of hail changed to say: *Will you stay engaged to me?*

"Well, my snowflake? Be my wife, my queen, my everything?"

I gazed at the prince who became my king, my love, the man who had transformed my lonely world.

"Brontes, I may not have chosen you when we first met, but I decided months ago that as long as you want me, I *will* be your wife and bear your children. That there would be hell to pay for anyone who tried to stop me."

He stayed kneeling on the ground, the anticipation of my reply apparent on his beaming face.

"Yes!" I giggled. "Of course, I'll stay engaged to you!"

Brontes rose from the grass, his silhouette a solitary shadow in the empty field, and he retrieved the ring from its box. With my left hand in his, cold metal brushed against my skin as he slowly glided the ring onto my finger.

"Perfect fit," he murmured.

I lifted my hand toward the night sky, and my breath caught in my throat as the moonlight illuminated the ring.

The exquisite thin band of black tungsten, scattered with micro diamonds, mirrored the vast expanse of the starry sky above us. Among the tiny flecks of stardust, the dark metal sparkled with an array of dazzling, color-shifting stones, each shard a perfectly unique fragment. Hints of sapphire and amethyst mingled and transformed into amber and magenta at the gentle caress of moonlight, as if the very essence of the cosmos itself had been captured in an ever-changing symphony of vibrant colors within this ring.

"Brontes, it's beautiful!" I exclaimed joyfully.

"I had it made for you," Brontes whispered as we admired the ethereal allure of the ring together. "It's called 'The Veil Nebula.'"

My eyes lit up with enthusiasm. "Like the supernova!"

He chuckled, knowing that I would recognize the name. "Yes, the supernova that inspired it. I want to give you the universe, and this is the closest thing."

Tears ran down my cheeks, overwhelmed by the beauty of his gift. I loved everything about it—the shining black metal, stronger than both steel and titanium like my Brontes, and the glittering jewels depicted all that I loved about the cosmos.

"It's so perfect, Brontes!" I threw my arms around his neck.

Brontes swept me up into his arms, twirling me in the air as I laughed and held onto him tightly. He set me back on my feet before capturing my lips in a passionate kiss.

A warm rain shower began to fall around us, and I realized Brontes had recreated the very setting of our first kiss. Our lips tangled together as droplets clung to our faces, and the warm rain streamed down our cheeks. Raindrops pattered on the ground, soaking through my thin dress and clinging to my skin as I pulled away from his kiss.

"Is this your doing?" I chuckled as we held each other, two drenched souls, just like before.

He shrugged underneath my arms, flashing a coy smirk. "I have no idea what you're talking about." Brontes smiled softly. His arms wrapped tightly around my waist as he gazed down at me with his gorgeous navy eyes. "I love you, Gwyneira."

"I love you too, Brontes. You're my dream now."

Our hands found each other, fingers interlacing as we stood with our soaked bodies pressed together but utterly content.

"I love the taste of rain on your lips," Brontes said roughly as he brushed off the wet locks of hair from my face.

I licked my lips at the sight of his saturated clothing over his enormous frame. His shiny dark hair clung to his chiseled face, water dripping down from it to the curve of his strong jawline. His rain-soaked shirt adhered to his sculpted torso, outlining every muscle beneath, sending an almost primal urge through me.

His dark smoldering eyes scanned my body with a hunger that mirrored my own. He growled low in his throat and claimed my mouth in a fiery kiss.

Our tongues met in a passionate, feverish dance, exploring and relishing each other as my hands roamed over his broad shoulders and down his back. The warmth of his rain-slicked skin seared through the damp fabric that separated us.

As the rain continued to pour down, I reveled in the sensation of his strong arms wrapping around me, the warm droplets caressing my skin like a thousand tiny kisses. I breathed in the scent of him, feeling completely lost in the moment.

He pulled me closer, his hard body against my soft curves. He hitched my leg around his hip, pressing his hardness into me.

"Brontes," I gasped, shuddering at the evidence of his arousal, desire flooding my senses.

"I need to make you mine, Princess," he growled.

With those words, Brontes scooped me up in his arms effortlessly, cradling me against his firm chest as we made our way back to the castle. I nuzzled against his neck, peppering kisses along his jaw. Each step up the stone staircase jostled my body against his muscular frame, only further stoking the fire within me.

When we reached our chambers, he kicked the door shut behind us and pinned me against the wall, kissing me fiercely. His hands slid under my soaked dress, caressing my thighs.

My hands found their way to the hem of his shirt, pushing the fabric up and off his broad shoulders. I raked my nails down his chest, eliciting a groan from him.

He grabbed the hem of my dress and jerked it over my head, before releasing my bosom from their constraints. He then made quick work of tugging my panties down my legs until they dropped to the floor, leaving me bare. I shivered as the warm air kissed my exposed flesh.

"Gods, Gwyneira, you're exquisite," he whispered, his eyes drinking me in as if he were seeing me for the first time all over again. "So perfect. Mine."

Brontes wrapped his arms around me and lifted me, carrying me to the bed. He laid me down gently, his eyes roaming hungrily over my body.

"I'm going to worship every inch of you," he said thickly while slowly unbuckling his belt and unfastening his pants as if he was about to punish me.

His pants fell to floor, and his erection sprang free, hard and thick. I whimpered at the sight of him in all his taut, muscular glory. His body was a work of art, honed to perfection.

He climbed on top of me, running his hands lightly over my curves, his fingers barely grazing my skin. His touch ignited every nerve ending with a scorching heat, eliciting a desperate mew from my lips.

"I need to taste you," he growled, before lowering his head down and burying his face between my legs. "You're so pretty here. So pink and wet for me."

Brontes' breath ghosted over my sex, making me squirm, before his tongue dragged a broad stroke through my wet folds.

"Brontes . . ." His name fell from my lips as I let out a moan, the sound vibrating around us.

My entire body tensed as his tongue swirled and lapped at my entrance, teasing and exploring as if trying to consume every drop of my desire. When he turned his attention to my nub, sucking it gently between his lips, a jolt of pleasure shot through my core, and I knew I was undone.

"Oh!" A strangled cry escaped my lips, my back instinctually arching on its own.

"You like that?" he asked, looking up at me with dark, hungry eyes.

I bit my lip, trying to stifle my moans as he alternated between slow, languid strokes and quick, teasing flicks. His talented mouth devoured me with single-minded intensity as my body coiled tighter with building pressure.

"Yes!" I hissed, my fingers gripping the bedsheets.

And without warning, he plunged two fingers into my slick channel, curling them to hit that perfect spot while his tongue continued its relentless assault on my most tender flesh.

"Ahh . . ." I panted, on the brink of ecstasy, the sensations threatening to overwhelm me.

"Come for me, Gwyneira," he gruffly commanded.

His words drove me over the edge until I shattered with a scream, my inner walls clenching around his fingers.

Ecstasy flooded my senses, leaving me breathless and trembling beneath him. I sank into the bed completely boneless in the aftermath. He kissed my inner thigh and withdrew his fingers, gazing at me with smoldering eyes and a satisfied smile.

His chiseled body glowed in the dim light of our chambers, taut muscles outlined against his tan skin. I bit my lip as my gaze traveled from his sculpted abs down to his manhood, hard and thick, straining for my femininity.

"I want you inside of me," I ordered firmly. "Now."

His eyes flashed like blue fire against a night sky, before he gave a devilish smirk. "When did my snowflake become so demanding?"

"You made me this way." I winked slyly. "You said you would give me everything. I want everything."

Brontes groaned as I wrapped my hand around his hard length. He rocked into my grasp, desperate for more friction. I guided him to my entrance and locked my legs around his waist, urging him forward.

With one hard stroke, Brontes thrusted deep into my welcoming heat with a throaty groan. He slammed into me with relentless force over and over again, stretching me deliciously wide while pushing ever deeper. Every thrust compelled my breasts bounce and quake to the beat of his powerful rhythm.

A wordless cry spilled from my lips at the sight of him in ecstasy as we raced toward sweet oblivion together.

"Fuck, Gwyn . . . I'm not going to last much longer," he grunted through gritted teeth.

"Come inside me, Brontes," I hissed, my nails digging into his shoulders as my own climax neared again. My inner walls clenched as tightly as they could around him. "I want all of it."

Brontes' body stiffened, and he grunted loudly, thrusting deep as he filled me with his release, overtaking us in a blinding wave of rapture.

We clung to each other, panting harshly in a tangled heap. Brontes kissed me tenderly, brushing the hair back from my face.

"I love you," he whispered, his lips curved into an affectionate smile.

I cupped his cheek in my hand. "I love you too."

He stared intensely into my eyes. "You are my heart," he declared. "My very soul. My queen."

My fingertips trailed over the rough stubble on his chin and the softness of his lips. The love in his midnight eyes could not have been any more vivid.

I tugged him gently toward me, pressing my lips against his.

"My king."

CHAPTER TWENTY-TWO

The morning sun bathed the terrace in a golden glow, warming the smooth stone beneath my feet. The soft breeze caressed my face, bringing with it the fresh scent of dew-kissed flowers. I settled into the plush cushion of a wrought-iron chair, admiring the serene beauty of the rolling green hills and patchwork fields of the Storm Kingdom below.

Conveniently attached to our bedroom, the terrace had quickly become my favorite place in the castle to enjoy the first hours of the morning. It was a secluded oasis, far removed from the chaos and darkness that once enveloped our lives.

Even though he was king now, Brontes and I still stayed in his chambers as our primary bedroom. Neither of us felt comfortable in his parents' former quarters, the official Royal Chambers. The ostentatious bedroom was too gaudy for our tastes and simply didn't suit our style.

We'd discussed repurposing the space as an art gallery or a second library.

I nibbled on the end of my pen as I reviewed the words of my letter to Fannar. My last letter, begging for his help before making the journey to Storm Castle, had gone unanswered. But of course, things had changed, and I wanted him to know about the happiness I'd found with Brontes.

The scents of pine and moisture still lingered from the snowfall I'd summoned the night before. Leaning back into the chair, my gaze drifted lazily overhead. The snow had long melted away, leaving a breathtaking cerulean blue sky in its wake, the vibrant hue dotted with fluffy white clouds forming intricate shapes and patterns.

The door slid open behind me. I didn't need to turn to know it was Brontes. His presence stirred the air, like the charge before a thunderstorm.

"There you are, snowflake," Brontes said gently as he leaned down to press a kiss to the top of my head. "Enjoying the view?"

"Always," I replied, tilting into his kiss. "I'll never tire of it."

"It is beautiful, isn't it?" His arm snaked around my shoulders, his breath hot against my neck. "But not nearly as gorgeous as you."

Warmth rose in my cheeks. Even after all these months together, his compliments still made me blush. I nudged him with my elbow, unable to keep the grin from my lips. "Stop it, flatterer."

"Guilty as charged," he smirked.

I twisted my head to meet his gaze, the corner of my lips quirking up. "You should know by now that I'm not easily swayed by your charms."

"Oh really?" His brows shot up in a playful challenge. He leaned closer and brushed his finger across my jawline, sending a tingle through my body. "Care to make a bet?"

I narrowed my eyes at him, a smile playing at the corner of my lips. "What kind of bet?" I asked, arching one of my eyebrows suspiciously.

He leaned in even closer, his hot breath tickling my ear. "If I can make you scream my name before breakfast, then you have to wear that slinky blue dress I like so much for the rest of the day."

I swallowed hard, unable to keep my face from growing warmer at the suggestion. His eyes twinkled with mischief, and it took all my willpower not to lean into him.

"And if I win?" I teased, trying to keep my voice steady.

He flashed me a grin before leaning in closer, his lips brushing against my earlobe. "Oh, I don't need to think that far," he said in a gruff, low grumble.

His hands slid around my waist and pulled me closer still, speeding up my beating heart. The hair on my arms prickled as he traveled the length of my throat and collarbone with his lips.

"Do you remember what I said when I took you for the first time?" His voice rumbled, nipping lightly at my neck.

I nodded silently, trying to hold myself together as heat filled my veins, his lips blazing like fire on my skin.

"I told you that you were mine," he growled before finally claiming my lips.

Brontes clutched the back of my head and imprisoned me in a passionate kiss, his tongue pushing its way into my mouth with unrestrained force that made me melt into him completely.

Finally, reluctantly, we pulled apart, and Brontes released me with a sigh. He rested his forehead against mine for a moment longer before taking a step back with a knowing smirk on his face.

I steadied my breath before looking into his eyes again. "You weren't wrong." I winked before smiling softly at him.

He gave an amused chuckle. "As much as I would like to continue this, we should really get going before the rest of the court starts to wonder what happened to us."

I nodded, letting out my own little sigh of regret.

Brontes looked down at the paper and pen on the iron filigreed table in front of us. "Are you almost finished with your letter?"

"I think so." I passed him the letter, ink still wet from where I'd hastily scrawled my name. "Tell me what you think."

My dearest brother,

Words cannot describe my happiness! The stories about the Storm Prince being a monster are false. Brontes is an amazing person who loves me very much. When he learned about my love of astronomy, he gave me "For the Love of Stars: A Study of the Cosmos" and built me an observatory!

Sadly, his parents destroyed the observatory, but we are building a bigger and more beautiful one in its place. I cannot wait to show it to you!

With the help of the castle staff, we overthrew his parents in a coup. Brontes is now the Storm King, and I will soon be the Storm Queen. We are looking forward to planning our wedding and coronation. Of course, I fully expect my big brother to be there!

I can also control my ice powers, so you can look forward to a snowy greeting when you come to visit, which I hope is soon!

How are your studies at the academy? Please let me know how you are doing.

Hope to see you soon,

Gwyneira

I watched as Brontes read the words I'd written, his eyes scanning back and forth in concentration. When he finished, he smiled at me.

"You told him about rebuilding the observatory." He grinned. "It's adorable how excited you are about it."

"Of course, I did! The new observatory is going to be amazing, and I can't wait to show it to Fannar when he visits. He'll be so impressed!"

"Hopefully, we'll hear back from him soon."

My heart twinged, remembering how Fannar still hadn't responded to my last letter. When I expressed concern about it before, Brontes insisted there could be any number of reasonable explanations for the delay.

Brontes comfortingly squeezed my shoulder, gently tucking a stray strand of my hair behind my ear. "So, do you think we should send this letter to the Ice Castle or Haven Academy?"

I tapped the pen against my chin, considering the options. "Well, I'm not sure when he'll go home for winter break or even how long the letter will take to there. Maybe we should send it to the academy just to be safe? If anything, it'll be waiting for him when he goes back to school."

"Sounds like a plan," Brontes agreed, nodding thoughtfully. "It'll be a nice surprise when he starts classes again."

"Yes!" I exclaimed, grinning at the thought of Fannar receiving my carefully crafted words. "He'll be so happy to hear from us."

Brontes smiled warmly as he sat down in the chair next to me. "Speaking of Haven Academy, I have some good news for you."

"What is it?" I asked, curiosity piquing as I set the letter down.

"I know you've always wanted to attend the academy." He took my hands in his.

"We already talked about this." I furrowed my brows, slightly confused. "It's okay. I want to stay with you."

"I know," he continued. "But since neither of us had the chance to attend Haven Academy, I reached out to the headmaster."

"About what?"

"I told her that as rulers of the Storm Kingdom, I want us to have the best, most well-rounded education possible. So, I've arranged to have a couple of professors come teach us here at the castle every semester!" He beamed proudly.

"Are you serious?" I jumped up, nearly knocking my chair over.

"I know it's not the same as being there, and it'll take us longer to officially graduate but—"

Before he could finish his sentence, I had already thrown my arms around his neck. "That's wonderful, Brontes! Thank you so much!"

He chuckled at my enthusiasm as he stood up to embrace me. "Perhaps you can still become one of the Enchanted Realm's leading astronomers, as well as Queen of the Storm Kingdom."

"Oh, Brontes." I buried my head in his broad chest. "This means the world to me."

Brontes held me close, his heart thundering under my ear.

"Anything for you, my snowflake, my queen. Always," he replied.

I tilted my head up, meeting his gaze. The adoration in his eyes conjured tears in my own.

How had I gotten so lucky? Once upon a time, the thought of marrying the Storm Prince had filled me with dread. Now, I couldn't imagine my life without this man who had so unexpectedly become my whole world.

Unable to resist, I pressed a soft kiss to his lips. Brontes made a low sound in his throat, arms tightening around me as he deepened the embrace.

A delicious warmth spread through me, setting my blood aflame all over again. I sank into him, my hands sliding up to tangle in his hair.

When our lips parted, he left me breathless as always. His warmth seeped into my skin, a delicious contrast to the cool morning air and my own naturally frigid skin. Our fingers intertwined, and I admired how perfectly our hands fit together.

As we stood there, enveloped in each other's love, a fierce determination took root within me. Brontes was my everything, and I knew that I would do anything for him. Our love was destined, written in the stars.

Together, we would build a kingdom founded on kindness, hope, and new beginnings. The world never seemed so full of excitement and possibility, and I eagerly awaited the journey that lay ahead. As long as we had each other, Brontes and I would weather any storm the gods threw our way.

EPILOGUE
HELENA

I rubbed my hands together vigorously, desperately trying to generate the slightest bit of heat. The entire fucking castle was made of ice. Yes, it's called the Ice Kingdom for a reason, but seriously?! I didn't even know such things existed outside of Disney movies.

Cupping my hands together, I blew an orange ribbon of flame into my palms, bringing some miniscule source of warmth to my frozen bones. As I glanced out the window, endless snowdrifts blanketed the landscape of this unfamiliar place. All I wanted was to see green grass again.

Things would be greener—warmer—if we'd gone to the Earth Kingdom for winter break.

I shook the thought away and reminded myself why I was really there. Because Fannar needed me.

He perched awkwardly on his bed, his face rigid and expressionless as he stared into nothingness. His elbows rested firmly on his knees with his fingers interlocked at the front of his face. His left foot tapped restlessly against the smooth floor. Tiny snowflakes hovered around him in the air, attempting to cocoon him in an icy aura.

Maybe *he* was the one freezing the room? As if it needed to be any colder!

"Fannar. Babe!" I pleaded with him. "We don't need more ice, please!"

Fannar's arctic blue eyes blinked up at me, like I'd disturbed his thoughts. "Sorry, Helena," he murmured. He stretched his back a little and huffed out a sigh.

The duvet on his bed crunched underneath me as I sat beside him, frosty from his powers spreading out around him.

"Still worried about your sister?" I asked.

Fannar nodded. His familiar icy expression revealed nothing, but I'd learned to read the tiny hint of emotion that his eyes betrayed.

"Every day that we're sitting around here, Gwyneira is trapped in the Storm Castle. Gods know what that monster is doing to her, Helena." He clenched his fists, and more ice collected on them. "We don't know if she's okay, if she's alive. Even Mother and Father don't know anything."

"How is it that they've seriously not checked on her once?" I snapped.

He shook his head. "Gwyneira is nothing more than a tool to them. Always has been." He paused and smiled humorlessly at me. "My parents would treat you the same way if they weren't so damn scared of you."

"That's me. Scary Fire Enchanted from the Unenchanted Realm." I grinned and shrugged, but Fannar hung his head again. I placed my hand on his. "Well, then, it's up to us to save her."

Fannar paused, contemplating my words. "It could start a war."

"So what?" I scoffed. "You're the future king of the Ice Kingdom. You have every right to rescue your sister if the prince is being cruel to her."

As the words left my mouth, I knew I had him. Fannar was always so soft-hearted when it came to Gwyneira. He looked at me with pleading eyes, silently asking me for permission to rescue his sister.

"What's the plan?" I smirked, knowing that I had won this battle. "I'm sure you've already thought about it."

Fannar's eyes lit up. "She has to be inside the Storm Castle. We can sneak in and look for her. Gwyneira doesn't have powers, or if she does now, she won't know how to use them. She's completely defenseless, so if we escape with her without anyone noticing, that would be best."

"If we're caught, the Storm Prince won't let her go without a fight." I slammed my fist down onto the palm of my other hand with a loud smack.

"Then we'll deal with him. We're two of the most powerful students at the academy. That has to count for something, right?"

I nodded, eying him cautiously. "But, by 'deal with him', you mean . . . ?"

Fannar's eyes and tone darkened. "If he resists, I'll kill him."

Gwyneira's and Helena's stories conclude in ***A Storm of Fire and Ice*** coming soon!

Turn the page to get a free novella and we'll let you know when *A Storm of Fire and Ice* is available.

LOVE THIS BOOK?

Want more fantasy & paranormal romance from Ariel Renner? Get a free book when you sign up for her email newsletter.

Get your free book now!

https://arielrenner.com/free-book

Printed in Great Britain
by Amazon

39281785R10155